Joyful the Morning

Also by Nora S. Unwin

POQUITO,
THE LITTLE MEXICAN DUCK

TWO TOO MANY:
A Halloween Story

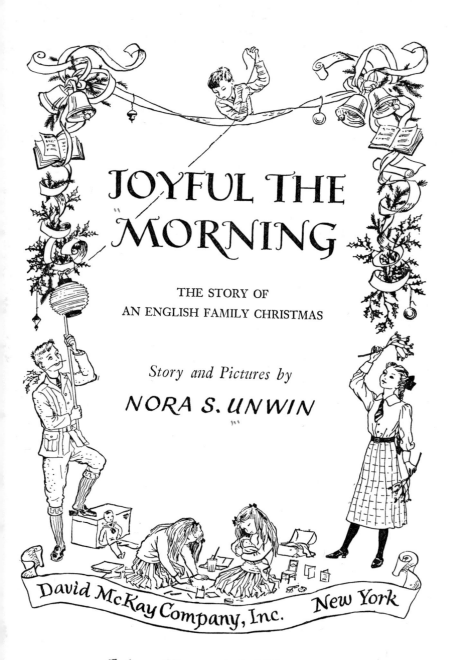

JOYFUL THE MORNING

THE STORY OF
AN ENGLISH FAMILY CHRISTMAS

Story and Pictures by

NORA S. UNWIN

David McKay Company, Inc.   New York

JOYFUL THE MORNING

MANUFACTURED IN THE UNITED STATES OF AMERICA

VAN REES PRESS   •   NEW YORK

Typography by Charles M. Todd

With *grateful joy*
remembering those in my childhood
who made each Christmas memorable

CONTENTS

Joyful the Morning

Wishes
AND PREPARATIONS

"Come along twins! Time to get up."

Mother looked into the twins' bedroom on her way downstairs. It was a dark winter morning, cold and foggy as usual. The room was dim and unheated.

"Already? Oh, but we *must* finish these," chimed two voices together.

"Finish what?" asked their mother, coming right into the room. "Gracious, you two! Aren't you frozen sitting there? It's high time you put some clothes on, and got some warm porridge inside you."

As usual, Patty and Penny had been drawing and painting. There they sat, eight-year-olds, as alike as two peas, on either side of a small table. Two smooth brown heads bent over their work, while a single candle flickered between them. Each had wrapped an eiderdown quilt, like a little nest, about her; woolly bedsocks covered their feet. Paints and pencils made a cheerful muddle on the table.

"Look, Mummy, don't you think Granny will like this? I made the border pink, because that's her favorite color." Penny held up a neatly executed design of holly, bells and flying ribbons.

"Yes, that's pretty. I'm sure she'll love it. But now you *must* hurry and clean up. Geoffrey has finished with the bath long ago. It's your turn now. And be sure to tidy your room, too. It doesn't look as though you'd touched the dolls' corner lately." Mother left the room.

"Buck up, you kids! You'll be late for your last day of school!" Geoffrey, taking the stairs at high speed and skipping the last three, reached the landing with a loud clatter, just outside the twins' door. He looked in.

"Pretty, pretty! Look at the pretty fairies," he teased.

"Go *away!* And we aren't doing fairies, so there!" The twins tried to hide their paintings. Penny flicked a wet brush at her brother.

"I say! Stop that! It's got paint on it." Geoff ducked.

"Of course it has," giggled Penny.

"Children, stop that nonsense, all of you." Mother called from below. "Geoff, come and start your breakfast. Girls, what did I tell you? Quick, now! Clean up! And don't let me have to tell you again." Mother sounded firm.

Penny waggled her brush in the tooth glass and shut the paint box.

"Don't," wailed her sister. "I need some more red." She furtively opened the paint box again.

Oh dear, thought Patty, why was it always time to do something else, just before you'd finished doing the thing that was most important? For Patty, that most important thing was always drawing. Nothing else quite took its place. Sewing was fun; dolls were special, but making pictures was pure bliss. They both loved it, Patty knew, but Penny had stopped now, and so ought she. Her conscience smote her.

Gazing in admiration at her own work, she rinsed her paint brush, tidied up, disentangled herself from her quilt and raced for the bathroom.

Washing had to be a sketchy affair, and she wrenched a button off her bodice as she dragged on her clothes. She longed to attend to the family of dolls who sat patiently round their yesterday's dinner table. The baby doll was still in bed. But Penny had already folded her nightie and gone downstairs.

Promising the dolls better treatment tomorrow, Patty kissed each cold china cheek hastily and ran to breakfast.

Dad was spreading butter on his last piece of toast as Patty kissed him good morning on the side of his cheek above his handsomely groomed mustache and slid into her chair. He remarked on her lateness, of course, and delivered a short sermon on punctuality. But his mind seemed to be more on catching his train to the city, and Patty noticed his blue eyes under the bushy eyebrows weren't really looking fierce.

Geoff gave her a smug look that said, "I told you so!"

Oh well, thought Patty, submerging her feelings in nice hot porridge with brown sugar on it, it wasn't the first time, and she knew, to her shame, that it would not be the last. But that Christmas picture she had just done was her best, so far, and she felt secretly pleased with the results. It must go to someone very special. She hadn't decided yet who that person would be.

Half an hour later, the twins were jog trotting toward the girls' school, satchels bumping on their backs, while Geoffrey, on his bicycle, headed in the opposite direction to the boys' school.

"Lucky pig, to be able to ride," gasped Patty. "If only *we* had bikes we wouldn't have to run like this."

"Well, he's two years older and there's only one of him."

"I don't suppose *we'll* get bikes till we're dreadfully old—not one *each* anyway."

They very well knew this side of being twins. Anything in twos was more expensive and they also knew the risks involved in sharing *one* of a thing between them. To *wait* was always the answer, and go on saving up.

"There'll probably be some Christmas money in our stockings, to help," suggested Penny.

"And think what else there may be for Christmas," whispered Patty excitedly. A secret glance passed between them. They both knew what they had wished for when they stirred the mince pie mixture two months ago. They grinned broadly.

It was fortunate that there were no serious classes in school that day. Exams were over, the school concert had been given; just the reading of marks, tidying of desks to be done and the final lecture by the Head. As the whole school sat in rows in the Assembly Hall, the twins' thoughts wandered considerably.

Christmas seemed to have been on the way, ever since that solemn ceremony in October with Mother and Cook, when they had all stirred the plum pudding and mince pie mixtures, and made their wishes. Now there were only four more days to wait, before they would know if their wishes had been fulfilled. But there were obligations, too, that filled Patty and Penny's thoughts. Would there still be time to finish that pincushion for Aunt Mary—and make a blotter for Aunt Milly? And there was still their Christmas play to rehearse with Geoff. The doll family must have their Christmas, too.

At last school was over. With carefree hearts and arm in arm with their best friends, the girls trooped out of the gate in cheerful groups. Three whole weeks of holidays lay ahead!

"It's early. We needn't go straight home yet. We'll see you to your house, Dora," suggested Penny.

"Then we'll see Jennie to hers," laughed Dora.

"And then we'll all see Patty and Penny back to theirs!" chimed in Jennie.

And so it went. This was a favorite bit of fun that they all loved on the last day of term. Their homes were only about ten minutes' walk apart. After several repetitions the

game became hilarious, and even the old road sweeper asked them if they'd forgotten where they lived. When they reached Jennie's gate for the fourth time, they heard her mother call her in to lunch. That reminded the other three that it was time to go home.

What a happy surprise Patty and Penny found when they pushed open their back door! Daddy had come home early from London and was free for the afternoon. He had changed from his dark city clothes and had on his comfortable old tweed jacket and knee breeches. The twins loved to see him dressed that way. The tweed had such a homey country smell. He was in jovial holiday mood, too.

"Well, twins! What about a walk to Kingsbury Market with me this afternoon?" he asked. "I expect there are some things that you need, aren't there, Mother?"

"Hurray! Yes, let's! And there's something *we'd* like to get, too." A meaningful glance passed between the two girls.

To MARKET,
TO MARKET

In less than an hour's time, two pairs of black-stockinged legs skipped along on either side of Dad's strong striding ones. Two red tam o'shanters, in place of the black felt school hats, bobbed up and down, two tongues were wagging, while the market basket swung from Penny's hand. And each girl listened to the pleasant sound of several coppers clinking in her coat pocket.

A visit to the old outdoor market with Dad in his Saturday mood was always an event. Walking there, by the river path, was an important part of it. Sometimes, if they were especially laden with packages, they might take the tram home. Few cars were to be seen in those days, and theirs was not a family that could afford a horse and carriage. There would not have been room, in their small garden, to keep even a pony and trap.

The morning fog had lifted. An orange sun was trying to shine through the wintry sky behind the tall elms on the far bank of the river. Four swans were sailing calmly downstream.

"How can they sit on that cold water!" exclaimed Penny.

"It doesn't feel cold to them," Dad replied. "The water can't penetrate their feathers and they have no blood in their legs to feel the cold. But look there! Do you see that V-shaped ripple on the water?" He pointed excitedly.

"Where?" Both girls stared wildly.

"There—higher upstream—see? That's Mr. Water-Rat with only the top of his nose above the water." Now Patty and Penny both spied him and were delighted.

"I'm surprised to see him out today," said Dad. "But maybe he felt like a little foraging."

Dad's sharp eyes could always be counted on to spot wonderful things during a walk—glimpses of an unusual bird, a well-camouflaged nest, strange plants or insects, or some wild creature's footprints. He loved to share his finds with his family. Tomorrow Jim and Janet, their elder brother and sister, would be home from their boarding schools; then there would be family walks all together. But this day, Penny and Patty felt was extra special, having their father all to themselves.

"Will there be time to feed the pigeons, Daddy?" asked Penny.

"Oh yes! Please let's!" joined in Patty. "I love to feel them perching on my sleeve, or sitting on my hat."

"We'll see," replied Dad. "I've quite a list of things to do here. But we'll go to Harrison's and you can probably get a pennyworth of grain and do your feeding while I choose my new chisel."

"Goody!" chorused the girls. It sounded hopeful.

Presently they left the river path and joined the main road into Kingsbury. Soon they were crossing the cobbled street to the old market place.

Open stalls, many with canvas canopies over them, stood close together. Cut flowers and winter plants on one, jostled potatoes, carrots, celery and strings of onions on the next. The noise and smell of the market place were both familiar. Shining blue-checkered mackerel and hunks of big fish and red crabs lay on slabs of ice, with yellow dried kippers hung in festoons above. There were baskets of cockles and winkles and pans of pink cooked shrimps on the front of the stall. Patty loitered to watch, with a slight shudder, the easy way in which the fishmonger, in his blue-striped apron and battered bowler hat, slapped his fish around, tossing it on the scales, then wrapping it in newspaper for his waiting customer. His hands looked red with cold and the fish scales stuck to them. Patty wrinkled her nose at the smell.

"Come on," she heard Penny calling, "or we'll lose Daddy. He's buying oranges over there."

The air seemed full of cheerful clatter. The stall keepers held a running conversation with the crowd, even while serving customers, each shouting the virtues of his wares and stamping his feet to keep them warm. The pigeons swept in flocks now and then from roof tops, or pecked in the debris under the stalls. An organ grinder was winding out his rackety tunes at a nearby curb, and horses and vans clattered by on the outside streets.

Penny slipped her arm through her father's as they joined him. He smiled down at her.

"How about some tangerines for a treat, eh?" he asked.

"Oo—lovely!" she replied, and then, a little hesitantly, "Do you think we might get a box of dates, too—a pink box, with the little blue flower in it?"

"Well, I don't know why not. After all, it *is* Christmas." Daddy clinked the change in his pocket, and fished out another florin.

It was wonderful not to be met with the usual reply, "That's too expensive." Today was different.

Soon Dad had to carry the basket, it was getting so laden. They even bought a bunch of mistletoe, some folding paper lanterns, and six glorious shining colored glass balls to hang in the hall. These Patty carried very carefully in their fragile box. But an awful moment came when she nearly dropped them.

"Look!" Penny had cried, clutching her arm. "There he is! Quick! Look!"

"Where? Look out or I'll break them!"

"There! Just getting on, outside the chemist's."

"So he is," said Dad. They all stood still to watch this always fascinating sight—the old man riding a high bicycle. He was a familiar though not frequent figure in the town,

and his ancient bicycle and mode of travel had an unfailing
fascination for the children. They gazed entranced.

"I'm glad I have my freewheeler," Dad observed. "But
he's a remarkable old chappie. Well, now for home. I think
we've done everything, haven't we?"

The twins looked at each other—the pigeons—evidently
Daddy had forgotten. Should they remind him? But it was
getting late, and seeing the old man on his "penny farthing"
bicycle had been a sort of treat, too. So they said nothing
about the pigeons. Suddenly Penny felt the coppers in her
pocket.

"We had meant to go to the sweet shop and buy a pink
sugar pig for Geoff," she said.

"Well, there's still two more days. I really think we'd better make for home," Dad decided.

Dusk was fast approaching. The shops were all lighted, the stalls had orange gas flares, and the street lamps threw halos about them in the damp air. Dad set a brisk pace toward the river road. Before long he stopped abruptly.

"Drat it! We never went to Harrison's, did we? And what about those pigeons? You two! Why didn't you remind me?" He looked from one to the other, his blue eyes twinkling. "I believe you were afraid to ask me," he chuckled. "Shall we go back?" The girls hesitated and exchanged glances.

"I'm getting awfully hungry," faltered Penny.

"And my feet are rather cold," said Patty.

"Well, how about stopping at that bakery ahead and picking up a Sally Lunn for tea instead? And maybe they sell sweets too."

Penny and Patty brightened immediately.

"Yes, let's, if you don't think the pigeons will mind?"

Daddy agreed that they were probably getting plenty of scraps anyway. So the stop at the bakery was made. Dad also bought a tiny miniature cottage loaf, two inches high, "for the dolls' tea," as well. And, joy of joys, they did sell sweets, too.

Patty and Penny scanned the shelves hopefully. "Do you by any chance have any sugar pigs?" their father inquired.

"Sorry, none in at the moment," said the pleasant fat woman in the white apron. "But wait a minute, I believe I have a few sugar mice left." She disappeared, soon to return with a square white box. "Yes, just a half dozen."

"Ooo, lovely." The girls smiled, gazing enraptured at the pink and white mice, with their black beady eyes and tails of string.

"Tuppence each. Shall I wrap 'em all together?"

"Please," said Patty. Now they felt satisfied. And somehow six mice looked better than only one pig.

The thought of this, and toasted Sally Lunn to come, buoyed Patty and Penny all the rest of the long walk home, while Daddy told them fascinating things about the water rat, and some of his bold tricks, and how the kingfisher has his nest at the end of a long tunnel in the riverbank, where the water-rat can't get his babies.

As she listened, Patty was thinking about the picture she had painted that morning. It was a snow scene, with children in bright caps and mufflers bringing presents, and knocking on someone's front door. She felt sure it was her best. Why was there so seldom snow in England, she wondered.

A REHEARSAL

THE REPEATED strains of "The Merry Blacksmith" could be heard, sometimes haltingly, from the drawing room, where Geoffrey was practicing the piano. Stranger sounds issued from the dining room—Penny sawing away at "The First Noel" on her cello. To Patty, on the floor behind her mother's armchair in the cosy little sitting room (carefully putting the last stitches into the needle book she was making for her mother's Christmas present) all this had the comfortable sound of home.

It would be her turn next, on her violin, and she dreaded leaving her warm corner for the other chilly room where no fire burned on the hearth. Besides, she still had another row of cross-stitch to do. Mother was sewing the fastenings on two new velvet dresses she had made for the twins to wear this Christmas. Patty felt excited inside.

"*Promise* you won't look, Mummy!" she urged, every time her mother moved or left the chair for something.

"You haven't any *idea* of what I'm making, have you?" she added anxiously.

Mother assured her, of course, even though a few weeks ago she had herself supplied Patty with suitable materials

from her scrap box. Soon Penny's practicing was over. She bounced in, closing the door behind her, and ran to squat by the fire and warm her cold hands.

"Your piece sounded much better tonight," said Mother encouragingly. "Now your turn, Patty. See if you can't get yours well enough, too, to play on Christmas night."

Patty left the room reluctantly, after she had tucked her sewing back into a crumpled paper bag and stuffed it under the book shelf. She knew she sounded worse than Penny, but playing the violin was still quite a novelty to her and she was determined to do as well as her twin.

At last they were all free.

"Now for our rehearsal," said Mother, "and I think we had better try on some costumes tonight. Do you all know your parts?"

It was traditional in their family for the children to pre-pare some dramatic entertainment for the grownups on Christmas night. Sometimes it was a real play. More often it was part of a favorite story dramatized. Once they had acted the Mad Tea Party from Lewis Carroll's *Alice in Wonderland*. Jim made a gloriously mad Hatter; Janet, with her long fair hair, had been just right for Alice. The March Hare had been Geoff's part, so the Dormouse had had to become two mice, his part divided between Penny and Patty, much to the amusement of the assembled rela-tives.

But this year Jim and Janet felt too grown up for such activities. So the twins were to be Tweedledum and Tweedledee, from *Through the Looking Glass*, while Geoff, nobly swallowing his pride, had agreed to be Alice.

"Fetch me the book, Geoff," said Mother, laying aside her needlework.

"These chairs can be the trees," announced the twins, pushing the furniture about.

"And I'll get the dish covers and things," called Geof-frey, clattering down to the basement kitchen. Mother fetched a big cardboard box.

"Look, I believe this old dress of Janet's would be fine for Alice." She held up a blue-checkered gingham. "And look what else I have for Geoff to wear." She produced some long tresses of golden hair.

The twins shrieked with laughter.

"Wait till he sees that!"

"Oh Mum," groaned Geoff, who returned at that moment, "I'll feel an awful chump in that rig-out."

"No, wait a minute," Mother said, adjusting the long hair over his thick mousy crop. "You'll make a beautiful Alice."

He really did look as pretty as any girl could wish, the twins thought, as they surveyed him. Meanwhile, they were struggling into old pajamas of the boys, stuffing themselves with cushions, and trying to conceal their hair under round school caps.

"I'm not *nearly* fat enough," said Penny, looking at herself in the hall mirror.

"What about *me* then?" giggled Patty, bouncing her large protruberance against her sister's middle and nearly sending her flying.

"I say, I need more stuffing!" Penny seized a long woolly scarf from the hat stand and wound it around her. "Look out!" And she came charging towards Patty.

A glorious bumping match ensued, the girls capering around and bouncing off each other's well-padded stomachs with shrieks of delight. Tweedledum and Tweedledee finally landed on the floor, weak with laughter, and had to be helped to their feet by Alice.

"If you'd only put as much energy into your tantrums in the play, Tweedledum," observed Mother to Patty, "that would be capital. Now come along, no more silliness! Let's begin."

The girls took up their stance.

"If you think we're waxworks..." began Patty solemnly, though her twin's arm around her neck tickled and made her want to laugh.

With a few hesitations the rehearsal went fairly well. But Patty kept forgetting Dum's "No how!" And Penny still needed prompting on the long verses of "The Walrus and the Carpenter." Geoff became bored, and they were all growing cross.

"You need to work at your cues more," Mother told them. "Let's go over this last part just once more. Then it will be time for bed."

"Oh, not bed yet," cried the twins in dismay. "There's lots more we've got to do this evening."

"But there's still tomorrow," replied Mother.

"I know, but Christmas is so near, and we've not made anything for Auntie Margery yet, and I don't know *what* to give her, either. And I wanted it to be something *special.*"

They both talked at the same time and were nearly in tears at the thought of this sad omission where their favorite aunt was concerned.

"Sssh, both of you," said Mother firmly. "And cheer up! I've got an idea. But I'll save it till tomorrow." She got up. "Let's pack up now and straighten the room. Fold your things together nicely. Don't you remember what old Nanny always used to say? 'Joy cometh in the morning.'"

Suddenly the words of Nanny's old hymn brought a cheering sense of confidence to Patty and Penny. Even the thought of having to go to bed wasn't so bad now.

Half an hour later after their bath as they sat by the fire, each with a bowl of warm, sweet bread-and-milk, they began to hum the old familiar tune, with its cheerful refrain.

> *"Joy cometh in the morning*
> *Joy cometh in the morning . . ."*

Yes, perhaps there would be time for everything tomorrow, after all—finishing presents, learning parts, and the dolls' Christmas party. The needle book was tucked under Patty's pillow, ready to finish when she woke up next day. But what *was* Mummy's idea, they wondered? Anyway, whatever it might be, it was sure to be a good one.

CHAPTER FOUR

TWO MANY COOKS

"MAKE SWEETS! What fun! Can we really?"

The twins greeted Mother's suggestion with shouts of glee.

"You can begin right after lunch when Annie is out of the kitchen. I'll help you get started."

"Bags I make toffee! Aunt Margery loves toffee," announced Penny.

When anyone said "Bags!" first, it always meant that person had won first choice. At this moment Patty did not mind.

"I'll make her peppermint creams, some pink and some white." Patty was pleased with her choice. She knew she was playing safe, because these didn't need any cooking, Mother had explained. But it would need careful judgment to make the right shade of pink.

At two o'clock they donned their overalls and went down to the kitchen.

"You'd better work on this end of the table, Patty," said Mother. "And Penny, you do your mixing near the stove. Remember, Patty, peppermint is a *very* strong flavor. You'll only need a few drops." And she reached down a tiny bottle from a top shelf of the cupboard.

Carefully Patty measured out the lovely pure white confectioner's sugar on the kitchen scales. Mother showed her how to sift it into her bowl and told her all the steps to take.

"Next you'll need the white of one egg."

"Oh," said Patty, apprehensively. To separate the white in an egg seemed an awesome undertaking.

"Want me to do it?" asked Mother, as Patty hesitated.

"I can do it for you," boasted Penny confidently.

"No, you can't—not any better than me!" Patty's courage returned with a rush. "I'll do it myself."

She picked up the brown egg and tapped it gently on the edge of the bowl. Nothing happened. She tapped again. A tiny crooked crack appeared.

"Harder," urged Penny. Patty tapped once more.

A spurt of egg white shot quickly into the bowl. Patty began, expertly, to open the crack further, as she had seen her mother do.

"That's right, just tip it to and fro and dribble the white out gradually," her mother directed.

This was the tricky part, but Patty's hand was steady. The white jellyish liquid began to fall in a fine stream. It was perfect.

Suddenly a streak of yellow joined the white.

"Help! The yolk's coming, too," groaned Patty. "I've ruined it!"

"Here, drop it in this saucer." Mother came to the rescue. "Fetch another egg and try again in a fresh bowl. This time, pour the whole, yolk and all, into your hand. Then you can let the white slip through your fingers."

Patty tried again. She got the top of the egg off safely, then tipped the contents into her palm. How cool and slithery the egg's inside felt! She shuddered and almost dropped it.

"Ugh," grunted Penny, watching intently.

Suddenly, with a little "plop" the white dropped free into the bowl.

"There!" grinned Patty in triumph. She placed the soft yellow ball of yolk with the other broken one in the saucer. "Poor little yolk, you've lost your jacket."

"Now please help me," demanded Penny.

So Mother turned her attention to the toffee making, while Patty progressed to stirring and mixing, adding drops of peppermint, hot water, and cream, with perhaps more taste-testing than was necessary. This part was fun.

"Remember, just be sure you keep stirring," Mother was saying, as Penny, armed with a wooden spoon, watched the butter slowly melting in the bottom of the saucepan. "Call me when it has thickened. I must see to something upstairs. Be sure you have your waxed paper ready, Patty, before you roll out."

Mother hurried away.

"It's all melted," announced Penny with satisfaction, a few minutes later. "Now for the treacle!"

How delicious, shining and brown it looked, trickling from the spoon! She made wiggly patterns with it all over the sea of butter.

"Next my sugar."

Then, round and round went the spoon. Penny felt efficient and important. No busted eggs or slimy whites to bother with here.

Patty was engrossed with rolling out her ball of white pasty sugar with the rolling pin.

"Aren't you going to make half of them pink?" asked Penny, glancing from the stove.

"Bother! Yes! I forgot." Hastily Patty scooped up half her flattened ball and returned it to the bowl.

By this time it was hard to make the cochineal mix well. The effect was pale and streaky.

"Oh dear, this looks horrid," she mourned.

"Try putting in more pink," suggested Penny.

"No, more hot water would soften it, I think." Patty ran for the simmering kettle. "But perhaps I should cut out my white ones first before they get too hard." She surveyed them anxiously.

"Here, I'll pour the hot water while you add a bit of pink," offered Penny helpfully.

"Well, only a little, mind." Patty uncorked the small bottle, but now her hand was shaking with excitement.

"Oh, that's too much—bother!"

"You could have it striped like that and pretend they are humbugs," suggested Penny.

"But I wanted a beautiful delicate pink."

Gradually a smell of burning began to permeate the air. Penny remembered in a flash.

"Oh, my toffee!" She flew to the stove. The bubbling mixture had thickened and stuck at the bottom. All Penny's strength could hardly move the spoon. "Help!" she called, "fetch my pan for me!"

Patty darted for the buttered pan, ready on the dresser. Scraping and struggling with a blunt knife as well, they managed to get a fair proportion of the dark brown glassy stuff into the pan, where it hardened in an odd, rocky shape. A goodly amount stuck fast to the bottom of the saucepan and refused to budge. It stuck to the spoon and knife, too, and almost defied licking. It tasted delicious, the twins agreed, even if the slightly burned flavor was undisguised.

"Is something burning?" Mother's voice called down.

"Not any more, Mummy." The twins looked guiltily at each other. "Quick! Put the saucepan to soak." Patty remembered just in time.

By now the pink peppermint mixture had hardened some more. So with a sigh Patty tipped in some more water, then more suger, and then re-mixed and rolled the white ones. Finally she got to the stage of cutting out the little circles with a silver serviette ring.

"Let's borrow Mummy's thimble and make some tiny ones for the dolls, as a surprise," suggested Penny.

"Yes, that would be fun, but only out of the scraps. I'll save these corners for them."

Penny went in search of the thimble, while Patty arranged her peppermint creams in neat rows. By the time all was done, some of the white ones looked distinctly gray, and a few pink ones were rather oddly streaked.

"But they taste like peppermint creams all right." Patty surveyed her handiwork with satisfaction. Packed in rows in a notepaper box, they would look quite professional, she thought.

"I think I'll pack my toffee in a salt tin," decided Penny.

CHAPTER FIVE

OFF TO GRANDMA'S

PATTY AND PENNY lay on their backs in bed, look-ing at the ceiling and singing at the tops of their voices.

"Joy cometh in the morning.
Joy cometh in the morning."

Joy indeed! The great day had arrived, and they were squirming with excitement inside, thinking of all that lay ahead. This year it was their family's turn to spend Christ-mas with Grandma at Glenmore.

Christmas eve, with the train journey to Grandma's, was "to-day" at last! Packing was mostly done, save the last minute things. The presents they had made *had* got finished somehow, and now, wrapped in plain brown paper and tied with white string, were safely tucked in the bottom of Mother's suitcase. They chuckled as they re-membered how it had needed Daddy and Jim's help to pry

Penny's toffee out of the tin, and hammer it into small enough pieces. At last, securely packed, it was on its way, with the peppermints, by H.M. Royal Mail to Aunt Margery in the north of England.

Janet had helped them write the label because she could print so small and neatly. What fun it was having Janet and Jim home again! The first few days always felt a little strange, but at least there were no squabbles. Jim and Geoff had hung the paper lanterns and the glass balls over the hall and stairway, with the maximum amount of buffoonery, which delighted the twins, of course. They had skipped around, giving plenty of advice, though scant help. Meanwhile, Janet had fashioned an artistic arrangement of mistletoe for the hallway.

"Why all this fuss? Who's going to kiss who, anyway?" Jim had teased. "No one's going to catch *me*, by jingo!"

"You never can tell," Janet had said as she mounted the stepladder.

There had been whisperings and secrets, too, and they had all been forbidden to go into the guest room, where certain strange packages had been glimpsed through the crack of the door.

The dolls had had their Christmas party. Jennie and Dora had each brought theirs to tea, and the miniature loaf, cut, buttered, and with colored sugar sprinkled on each slice, had been eaten with ceremony.

"It's a pity we can't take Robin and Dick, or even our baby dolls with us," said Penny, "but I know there's no room to pack them, and Mummy says she'll need our hands to help carry things."

"Yes, we'll have our violin and cello to carry too, won't we?" Patty remembered. "I hope they won't feel lonely," she added, propping herself on one elbow, and looking at the group of dolls, sitting in various positions round a small table in the far corner of the room.

The doll family was the twins' particular joy. To Patty and Penny the dolls were real children upon whom they lavished much motherly attention, particularly when school activities did not interfere. Now they felt momentarily sad at forsaking them. But they decided that they might squeeze into their pockets two miniature teddy bears ("their children's toys") to take with them in place of the family.

"And you know," added Penny meaningfully, "there *might* be . . . ?"

"You never know!" agreed Patty, grinning. "Anyway, I'm sure they'll all be happy. They've got their little surprises to open, after we're gone. Look, Dick is holding his parcel of peppermints as if he could almost smell what's in it."

"Ssh," said her sister, "or he'll hear you."

Even the hateful ordeal of putting on clean underclothes when it *wasn't* Sunday seemed less irritating than usual. Penny and Patty tugged and pulled at their woolen combinations to make them feel less prickly. Later, with her tiny teddy in one pocket, a folded sheet of paper and pencil stub in the other, Patty still had a vague feeling in the back of her mind that something had been forgotten. She mentally ran over her list of Christmas gifts. Nothing had been left out, as far as she could tell.

At 11:45 sharp, the bags were in the hall, labelled and ready, for the "outside porter" who came from the railway station to wheel them on his barrow. While Mother attended to last minute details, Dad was giving orders.

"Jim, you carry the lunch basket. Geoff, take my field glasses. Twins, can you manage your instruments? They *could* go with the porter, you know." The girls shook their heads. "Well, Jim can take your cello half way, Penny. Come along then, we may as well start ahead and get the tickets. See you at the station, Mother. Tell Janet to hurry up."

They walked the quarter mile to the railway station, with the porter trundling his barrow a little ahead of them. Geoff, whose passion was steam engines, asked if he might sprint ahead to see the big Cornish Express go through at twelve o'clock.

"All right," said his father, "but be *sure* you are on Number Three platform by ten past."

Patty walked proudly beside Jim, with a little skip now and then to keep up. She adored having her big brother home from school, even if she did feel a little shy of him at first. He seemed taller and stronger every time. Jim was fifteen, but he was fun.

To the twins, Janet seemed almost grown up. She was sixteen and inclined to want to keep them in order. She

was neat and meticulous, and often thought Mother let the twins run too wild.

"But she needn't think she can boss *us*. We're two against one," they would wickedly confide to each other, after some family skirmish. Yet they really loved and admired their pretty elder sister, as well as her dainty personal belongings.

At 12:17 their train to the south pulled in, puffing and hissing. The crowd of passengers surged forward but the family waited while Dad found the guard to show them the empty compartment that had been reserved for them. Small bags were lifted to the rack and the two large cases put in the guard's van. Penny and Patty each dived for a corner window seat.

"Steady on, you two! You might wait for once, to see if anyone *else* would like a corner seat," reminded Janet.

"Would *you?*" asked Penny, pretending to look surprised. Then she added, "But, you see, our tiny teddies want to look out."

Neither twin offered to budge. Mother was preoccupied.

"Where's Geoff?" she asked suddenly. "He was with us a minute ago."

Anxiously she scanned the platform. No blue school-capped head was in sight. Geoff had been there on Platform Three when she arrived. Dad was busy tipping the guard, who already had his green flag tucked under his arm.

"Ed!" Mother called frantically, "where's Geoffrey?"

"Silly young idiot," remarked Jim. "I bet he's watching the trains somewhere. I'll go and find him." He jumped onto the platform, giving a shrill whistle, and was off like a streak of lightning.

Penny and Patty, with noses glued to the window, felt real qualms for their brother. Where could he be? He was almost *never* late for things.

"How many minutes can you hold her?" Dad asked the guard anxiously. "My son can't be far away. But I do apologize for this delay."

Watch in hand, the guard shook his head slowly. "Only another thirty seconds, sir. We're running behind the time-table a bit already."

Just as Dad was planning to stay behind and come on the afternoon train, racing footsteps could be heard over the foot bridge, and Jim and Geoff fairly tumbled down the steps and leaped into the compartment. Dad jumped in after as the train began to move.

"Thank heavens! Just in time!" gasped Mother. Janet moved up to make room for her brother.

"What on earth were you up to?" Dad demanded, looking sternly at his younger son, who had flopped onto the seat, panting wildly. "You knew our train left at twelve twenty-one."

"I ... it ... I didn't mean ..." Geoff began, between gasps, his cheeks flushed and eyes popping.

"Give the child time to get his breath," said Mother. She was just thankful to have the family all together again.

"Well?" said Dad, presently.

"Yes," said Geoff. "I did know, and I did come over to the platform at ten past. But then the twelve-five to London was late, and I wanted to see if it was being pulled by Sir Galahad. I thought there'd be time, and—and—" his eyes shone—"and it was!"

This was indeed a prize, another name and number to enter in his record, one of a new series of locomotives which all bore names from the classics. Penny and Patty could see by Geoff's face, that whatever Dad's reprimand, nothing could rob their brother of this private victory.

"First things first," Dad was saying. "To catch *this* train was the most important, and if it hadn't been for Jim, and the guard kindly holding the train, you'd have been left behind!"

"I'm very sorry," muttered Geoff meekly.

"Sorry isn't enough. See that it doesn't happen again." Then Dad turned his attention to other things.

Though it was only a two-hour journey to Grandma's, the train trip was always a big event. On the way, the family ate sandwiches from the picnic basket with biscuits, an apple and a square of chocolate each, to top off their lunch.

"I'm thirsty," announced Penny.

"Never mind. It won't be long before you can have a drink at Granny's," replied Mother.

There were familiar landmarks to look for and new things to see, as the leisurely train chugged its way through the soft green wintry countryside, stopping at several towns and villages, and waiting twenty minutes at one junction for an express to pass through.

Geoff was knowledgeable about all these events and, quite recovered from his misdemeanor, kept them all informed regarding gradients, signals, and the engine's speed.

Mother and Janet packed away the remains of lunch, while Patty and Penny propped their diminutive teddy bears on the window ledge and explained to them in whispers the passing scene. There was even time to rehearse "The Walrus and the Carpenter."

At last, after a long slow climb, and a giddy descent almost reaching thirty-five miles per hour, the train ground to a stop in Glenmore Station, and there on the platform was Uncle Gerald to meet them.

CHAPTER SIX

EXPLORATIONS

THE OLD panelled front door, with its big brass knocker, swung open, and Maggie, fresh and smiling in her white starched and frilled apron, greeted them all. Pattering feet could be heard in the passage. Aunt Milly came quickly through the hall, her blue eyes dancing behind her spectacles.

"Here you all are, and wonderfully punctual! The train must have been well on time! Did you have a good journey?" She gave them each a swift light kiss, then, chatting, laughing, asking questions all the while, she led the way upstairs, and explained that Granny was still resting. Dad and the boys and Uncle Gerald saw to the luggage.

"Will we be in the blue room, I wonder?" Penny whispered to Patty, as they climbed the wide shallow stairs with their handsomely carved banisters.

"Oh, I hope so! And by ourselves, too!" returned Patty.

Everything smelled of fresh polish and hyacinths. The dark oak panelling in the hall reflected the low afternoon sunlight. Under their feet the carpet felt thick and luxurious after the rather threadbare ones at home. Sprays of evergreen decorated the many pictures on the walls and branches of holly and ivy hung from the mounted antlers over each doorway. The twins were dazed with delight.

"Your mother and father will sleep there, in the room next to Granny, with Geoffrey in the dressing room," Aunt Milly was saying. "Now, up we go to find your beds!"

The top flight of stairs in the fine old Georgian house was very different, steep and winding. There was a handrail of rope on one side to hold onto.

"Here we are," smiled Aunt Milly, entering a large, low-ceilinged room. "The blue room for the girls. Do you like that?"

"Lovely!" the twins chorused. "Bags I sleep by the window!" and with this favorite expression they both ran forward, and tried to commandeer the single bed.

"No, I think that bed should be Janet's," said their aunt hastily. "I'd planned for you two to share this double bed. Unless, of course, Janet prefers to sleep with one of you?" she added.

"She *never* would!" Penny declared. They knew their sister would be horrified at such an idea, since she valued privacy.

"She'll probably wish she had a room to herself," whispered Patty. "So we'd better look out." She patted the big bed. "This is nice and soft, much softer than our beds at home."

"Is there a bolster?" asked Penny politely.

"Yes, why?" Aunt Milly looked puzzled.

"I just wondered," said Penny. But Patty knew why she asked. It was a necessary safeguard to put between them inside the bed. Even at Christmas time, they could not be sure that they might not get into a frightful squabble. They were still not beyond kicking and fighting if a real argument began. Each calmly recognized this as the worst side of being twins. However much you loved each other, and they knew they did, fighting was still a part of it, too.

When Janet learned the sleeping arrangements, she took it surprisingly well, the twins thought. She insisted, however, on taking charge of the candle and matches, and the clock, then begged Mother to rule that Christmas morning should not begin before 6:30 A.M.

"And Mother, please tell the twins they've got to do as I say, and not kick up a row," she urged.

"That's right," said Mother, who had come upstairs to help unpack their things. "No opening of stockings till Janet gives you the word, and promise me you'll be good about it, and try to be quiet."

Under protest, the twins agreed.

"Hullo, twins! You're lucky being in the blue room!" Geoff was checking up on everything. He ran across the room to look out of a window. "You can see the whole town from here."

Indeed, the wide view of old mossy slate and red-tiled roofs, branching chimney pots, gables and casements was one of the fascinations of the blue room. Beyond, wooded hills rose to the grey sky. On the garden side, you could look down on the hundred-year-old mulberry tree, twisted and huge, now propped up in several places and held with iron bands.

"Come on, twins!" cried Geoff suddenly. "Mum, may we explore the garden before tea and see if old Dobbin is still there?"

"Yes, I think you have time for a quick run round. But don't get into anything messy. Remember, you've all got on your good clothes." She handed the girls their red tams.

With a joyful clatter the three made for the stairs.

"Put your coat on, Geoff," Mother called, as she went down after them.

Janet was glad to be left alone to do her own unpacking in peace. She proudly shook out a new silk dress that she and Mother had bought two days ago. Its texture thrilled her.

In the early winter dusk the big garden seemed twice as exciting. The branches of the mulberry tree, bare of leaves, nearly touched the ground in places, forming a latticed tent. The tiny box hedges were neatly trimmed. Some Christmas roses were blooming in a sheltered corner. The tennis court looked misty and endless. Between tall pine trees and thick shrubs, winding paths lost and found themselves mysteriously. The air was damp and heavy with the smell of leaf mould.

To the twins, Granny's garden always felt enormous. It actually had a hill in it, where a wide gravel path dipped down toward a little woodland. This was an exciting place to race with the old mail cart (the ancient vehicle in which aunts and uncles, when babies, had ridden!). Jim usually acted as the prancing steed, Geoff as the footman, while Penny and Patty, sitting on the open seat, clung to the sides as elegant, but sometimes nervous, lady passengers.

"Do you remember that time when it nearly tipped over?" recalled Patty, as they reached the bottom of this hill.

"Yes, I do. It was right here," said Geoff. "And you cried."

"I *never!*" protested Patty stoutly, though, thinking back, she remembered she had come pretty near to tears of fright.

Now, looking up, under the tall pines, this far corner

of the garden felt positively spooky. She studied the pattern of branches and needles above her. What was that thick bunch of sticks and leaves up there? Was it a squirrel's nest, perhaps?

Suddenly she realized that her sister and brother had gone ahead. She felt all alone in the great garden. A momentary panic seized her. She couldn't even hear their voices. She started to run.

At that moment a great grey shadowy thing appeared noiselessly out of the dimness above and went "woo-o-o-sh" past Patty's face. She stopped in her tracks, heart beating wildly.

"Penny! Geoff! Where are you?" she tried to call loudly but her throat felt dry. She knew they would never hear. They must have reached the stables by now. A curious snuffling sound seemed to be coming from nearby. Patty dared not move. She listened intently. Then a raucous shriek suddenly split the air above her.

Patty took to her heels and fled up the path, not daring to look behind.

"What on earth's the matter with you? You look like a dying-duck-in-a-thunderstorm," exclaimed Geoff, as Patty, white-faced and panting, gained the safety of the stable yard, where comforting lights streamed out from the kitchen window.

"No-n-no!" stuttered Patty, "but there's something *horrible* down there in the trees. It shrieked at me and I felt it near my face."

"You baby! That was just an old screech-owl. I heard it, too," replied Geoff, as he wrestled with the padlock on the old barn door. It wasn't locked but the hook was stiff and hard to get out of the ring. Now the door itself seemed stuck. He tugged harder. Suddenly it gave way. The heavy door swung open, knocking Geoff backward, where he sprawled on the damp cobblestones.

"Ha! Ha! Baby yourself!" giggled Patty, quite restored to herself by this unexpected but comic misadventure.

"Here, let's wipe you off," suggested Penny more help-fully, inspecting the large muddy smear on the back of her brother's coat.

"Oh, it's only wet. It'll dry up," replied Geoff, brushing himself off casually and starting to march ahead into the stables.

There was a musty smell inside. Only garden tools, an old bike and the wheelbarrow lived there now, and an odd assortment of discarded objects. Yet the old smell of horse and hay still lingered in the rafters. In Grandpa's day the stables had housed a real horse and carriage. Penny wished she had known it then.

"There he is!" exclaimed Geoff, who had been prowling into far corners. "I see Dobbin!"

Sure enough, from behind a large lawn roller, the rump and back legs of a big rocking horse were visible.

"Dobbin!" the twins cried together. They all ran over to the corner, and with difficulty dragged the heavy crea-ture onto the open floor. He was, alas, tail-less, and almost maneless now; his dappled paint was faded and scratched, and there was a bad crack down one leg. But the proud carriage of his head, the distended nostrils, and the glint in his glass eyes all seemed to say, "I'm still good for a few miles yet!"

Dobbin had always held a fascination for them, though secretly the twins, who had no animals of their own, were really a little scared. He seemed so tall, just to sit on his back had always been thrill enough. They would watch with awe when Jim mounted and plunged to and fro. Geoff, however, felt braver and taller himself this year.

"How about a ride? Bags I ride first, because I spotted him first," he said, testing the rhythm of the great rockers. "Here, give me a leg up, one of you! And mind your toes!"

"Dare you?"

"Do you think you'd better? You've got your good knickerbockers on, remember."

The girls hesitated, in no eagerness to rob him of a first turn, but longing to try too, *perhaps*.

"Oh, come on!" Geoff gave a jump, grasping the wooden neck and trying to throw his leg over. There was an ominous cracking sound. He dropped back.

Just then a voice was heard calling from the house. "Geoffrey! Twins! Are you there? It's time to get ready for tea." Footsteps, and Uncle Gerald appeared in the stable doorway.

"I thought I'd find you here. Looking at old Dobbin? I'm afraid he needs a bit of repair before he's safe for riding. But perhaps your father and I can strengthen that leg for you in the next day or two. We'll have to see."

So Dobbin was pushed back into his shadowy corner, and they all trooped off toward the warm lights of the house.

CHRISTMAS EVE

ALTHOUGH it was not yet Christmas day, tea at Granny's was like a party. Penny and Patty changed into their new velvet dresses under Mother's supervision. She tied silk navy ribbons on their smooth hair. Janet had also changed from her blouse and skirt into her Sunday gabardine.

"Tomorrow we'll put on your pink satin ribbons," decided Mother, "and we'll save the new bronze slippers for Christmas day, too."

The little girls looked at each other approvingly, stroking the dark blue velvet, with the pink and blue embroidery on pockets, neck, and cuffs. Janet also approved. A mirror was unnecessary for the twins as neither doubted both looked the same. And anyway, Janet was in front of the long glass carefully adjusting a large black ribbon bow at the back of her head. Then she brushed out the long mane of fair hair below.

"Are those *real* silk stockings you've got on?" asked Patty admiringly.

"Of course," replied Janet with pride, though this was her very first pair.

"And we've got silk embroidery!" chimed the twins. They beamed with pleasure.

"Mummy, you are clever!" And each taking a hand of hers, they all went down to tea together.

Patty and Penny always felt awed at the decorous atmosphere, and the presence of a good many aunts and uncles, also a few older cousins who had arrived to celebrate the holiday. Their darling little Granny, always so dainty and rosy-cheeked, sat at the head of the long table in her tall-backed oak chair with the carving on it.

The twins ran to greet her. Granny's kisses were like no one else's. "Like silk thistledown," Patty always said. Granny's cheeks felt like silk, too.

She wore a grey satin dress with a soft white shawl over her shoulders, and on her head a tiny frilled net cap, trimmed with violets. Patty thought she looked like a queen. She pictured herself wearing just such a little crown when she was a grandmother. She would have forget-me-nots in hers, and wear a blue shawl.

There were beautiful white chrysanthemums and holly in the center of the table. The heavy wool curtains had been drawn, as it was now dark outside. Aunt Milly sat behind the big silver teapot at the other end, with an array of cups and saucers all around her, every one in different colors, but in the same shape, with gold rims. This harlequin set always fascinated the twins. It was fun to watch the cups and plates getting rightly matched to everyone round the table.

When all the thin bread and butter, toasted scones, jam sandwiches and rock cakes were finished, and even Geoff could not find room for one more chocolate biscuit, the grownups still sat over their cups of tea, talking and exchanging news. Granny gave Patty and Penny an understanding nod and they slipped away from the table. Penny ran to her chair.

"May we play the musical box, if we are very careful?" she whispered.

"Certainly, but perhaps Geoffrey will have to help you wind it," smiled Granny.

"No, I'm sure we can." Penny joined her sister at the door and they closed it politely after them.

They raced up the wide flight of stairs to the drawing room. This was the moment they loved. First of all, just being alone in this pretty room was a treat. It was fun to walk all around and look at everything carefully. Everything was as they remembered. The gold ornamental clock, with little people round it; the Dresden china shepherdess at one end of the mantel, and the shepherd calling to her at the other. A big feathery fern stood in a plant stand; blue hyacinths in a bowl scented the room. The fire burned brightly, flickering on an old-fashioned fire screen that stood nearby, embroidered with fancy fruits. Yes, and the two funny cushions (or were they footstools?) shaped like two tabby cats were also there in the corner.

In a glass case, near the piano, were all kinds of fascinating treasures: shells, trinkets, fossils, little ivory carvings, keepsakes brought from abroad or collected by Grandpa, whom they had never known.

Patty and Penny knew these were precious, to be treated with the utmost care. It did not occur to them to open the glass doors, or to touch the delicate china arranged on a small table by the window.

For a while they sat cross-legged on the hearth rug, each cuddling a cat cushion, momentarily charmed into silence by the dancing flames, the rumble of voices below, and the magic of the moment.

"I wonder what the dolls are doing now? I *hope* they are having a nice time," Penny murmured.

"I hope they haven't eaten *all* their peppermints yet," replied Patty.

"Well, the toffee would take them longer. I gave them all the broken crumbs and chips."

Somehow they still liked to believe that their dolls came alive and did things on their own, especially when their mothers were away.

"P'raps they'll have a little dance tonight?"

"Oh yes, a dance, that'd be nice. A dance! Why don't *we* have one now?"

"The musical box!" they exclaimed. "We forgot it!"

Together they ran to the cabinet behind the big armchair. There, in its usual place, on the Chinese embroidered cloth, stood the old musical box. Favorite of three generations, it could still tinkle forth its melodious tunes, with a familiar little hiccup and shudder before the opening chords of each piece.

Carefully Penny wound it up. Then Patty raised the lid and set the lever for starting. A second, inner lid had a glass top, so one of the joys was to watch the works, the way the various cogwheels fitted so perfectly, and to see the metal tines as they lifted and dropped over the tiny spikes on the slowly revolving drum.

For a while, the twins watched, fascinated. When it came time for "The Blue Danube Waltz," they could keep still no longer. Patty bounced into the middle of the room.

"Let's dance!" she cried, holding her arms out to her twin.

Swiftly and smoothly they began twirling around the room, practicing all they had learned in their dancing classes, to avoid the furniture. The firelight flickered on the walls, glinting from the pictures, transforming the room into a grand ballroom, in their imagination. They could picture themselves elegant ladies in a castle, dancing before a king. Then the waltz ended.

The musical box changed to a gay polka.

Penny broke away from her sister to execute some wild figures on her own. Patty did likewise—pirouettes, spins and high kicks. The tune was deliriously happy. Suddenly, one of Penny's high flings went too near the table by the window, the tip of her toe touched the edge of it. A little china bowl toppled, rolled, struck the window ledge, and broke in twenty pieces on the polished boards below.

The dancing stopped instantly. Patty rushed to turn off the music. Penny, her face red, and eyes fast brimming with tears, knelt to pick up the scattered pieces. Patty helped.

"If only it had fallen on the carpet," she whispered. She had a sick feeling in her middle. It might just as easily have been her own toe that had done it.

"How *awful!* Whatever shall we do? And on Christmas Eve, too." Penny was sobbing.

"I know, and these china things are terribly special, I'm sure!"

"What will Granny say?"

"I don't suppose any punishment could be bad enough.

Perhaps we won't get any presents from Father Christmas now? And we'll have to tell Granny."

"But I *can't* go down now, and tell her with all the others there. I *can't* do it," sobbed Penny. "And what'll we do with the pieces?"

"Here, let's put them in this dish. We *might* be able to mend it," suggested Patty. "And you could tell her tonight when we say good night."

"No," groaned Penny miserably, jabbing her knuckles into her eyes and sniffing hard. "I couldn't wait that long." Patty proffered a hankie.

"I think I'll go and wait in the hall, then perhaps I can tell Granny as she comes out from tea," Penny resolved.

"I'll wait with you." Patty, feeling equally guilty, really admired her twin's courage. She knew how awful she felt. But since Penny had actually done the deed, they both knew, in all fairness, she must be the one to tell.

With beating hearts, and a sinking feeling inside, they sat on the stairs, waiting, listening.

Finally, after a burst of laughter, they heard the family rising, and chairs being pushed back.

The door clicked, and Geoff, standing like a proper little gentleman, was holding it open for the grownups. He caught sight of his sisters but mercifully said nothing.

Granny came first, and by the time she stepped into the hall, leaning on Daddy's arm, Penny, stricken-faced, stood before her. Patty, whose courage failed her at the last minute, retreated higher up the stairs, and watched, anxiously, through the banisters.

Her sister's voice was so quiet that she could not really hear the dreadful confession. But she saw Granny bend down, whisper something in Penny's ear and, smiling, give her a pat on the shoulder.

With a heart immeasurably lightened, Penny walked sedately up the stairs behind her father. She slipped her

hand into Granny's and the three of them entered the drawing room together. Patty hovered near the door.

Penny showed her grandmother the broken pieces in the little dish, and her tears welled up again.

"Never mind, it was just an accident. We'll think no more about it. We can't have any sadness at Christmas time. Edward," said Granny, turning to Daddy, "put the pieces in that drawer for now. But I don't believe it will be worth mending. It's had a long enough life already," she added brightly.

"You know," said Dad, his eyes twinkling at Penny, "this was really a Chinese cup, that's why it had no handle. And if I remember rightly, it was I who broke the saucer when I was a kid. Didn't I, Mother?"

Granny nodded, smiling. Penny began to giggle through her tears. To think of Daddy smashing china! She dried her eyes and gave Granny a hug.

"You'll tell me what I can do, won't you?" she whispered.

"Yes, but we'll wait till after Christmas, dear. Now run along, and ask Maggie to bring up some more coal for the fire."

Gratefully, Penny ran from the room, as the rest of the family arrived upstairs. Later she and Patty sought refuge on the upper flight of stairs, to avoid questions for awhile.

"What did she say?" asked Patty anxiously.

"I don't think I'll tell you," replied Penny slowly. "It's a sort of secret with Granny, but she was awfully decent about it. It was only half a cup and saucer, after all. And isn't it funny? It was Daddy who broke the saucer years ago!"

"*Did* he? Oh, don't be mean. *Do* tell!"

"If you hadn't run away, you'd have heard," was all Penny would say.

Yes, it served her right, and Patty knew it. But she felt desolate, all the same, to be left out. Usually they shared any secrets with each other.

"Hey, twins, where are you?" Geoff's voice came from the landing. "What about a game of tiddly-winks? You coming?"

The remainder of the evening passed smoothly. No mention was made of the accident by anyone. Janet played the piano for Granny. She was doing really difficult sonatas now, and sounded wonderfully professional, the twins thought. They felt thankful that their turn would not come till tomorrow.

There was a loud knock on the front door below, and Maggie soon came up to announce, "Please, madam, it's the carol singers, Mr. 'Awkins' group, madam. Shall I ask them to come in?"

"Oh, by all means," Granny said. "I think, if they will sing to us in the hall, some of us can listen from here. Please leave this door wide open, Maggie."

"May we go down and see them?" begged the twins.

"Certainly," was the reply. So the girls and Geoff sat on the bottom step of the stairs, where they were soon followed by Jim, Janet and others.

Quite a crowd of ladies and gentlemen filled the hall, all muffled in warm clothing, with song books in their hands. Mr. Hawkins sounded his tuning fork and the singing began.

This was *real* music, Penny realized, all in parts, and far better than the choir in their church. She was enthralled. Patty listened intently too, watching the interesting faces and their expressions as they sang. How different, thought Penny, from the cracked or shrill voices of children at home, who had been singing from door to door, earning pennies for at least two weeks. But one night, a lone little boy had sung all by himself, and very sweetly too. So Dad had pulled out a sixpence for Penny to give him. She would never forget his unbelieving joy, as he rubbed the coin on his sleeve.

"Coo! A tanner! Thank yer, miss. 'Appy Christmas, miss." And he scuttled off into the dark.

Everyone was sorry when the singing ended. They applauded warmly. While Mr. Hawkins went up to the drawing room to receive Granny's congratulations, coins clinked into the tin box that was passed around "for the hospital," and Aunt Milly produced a plate of goodies for the members of the chorus.

Later this evening, the whole family sang carols to Janet's accompaniment. Pictures of the manger, shepherds, stars and snowy hillsides filled Patty's mind as she sang. Suddenly, with a pang, she remembered something. Her picture, her special Christmas picture! She'd left it behind. She knew she had never taken it from the back of the drawer where she had kept it secret. And I meant to give it to Granny, she thought desperately. It was too late now.

"But I thought you were giving your woven paper mat to Granny?" said Mother, when Patty confided in her later, while being tucked into bed.

"Yes, I am, but this was sort of extra, because it was my best."

"Well, I'm sure Granny will be very pleased with the mat, darling. I wouldn't worry for now. Try to go to sleep, there's good girls, and each remember to keep on your *own* side of the bolster."

With a good-night hug and kisses, Mother left the room.

Oh Joyful
THE MORNING

THE LAST flickering flames of the fire had died and only the faintest red glow dimly lit the center of the blue room. Penny sat up. Surely it was morning. She must have been asleep for hours.

"Thank goodness you've waked up," said a weary voice beside her. "You were snoring terribly."

"I *wasn't!*" retorted Penny.

"Yes, you were. I've been awake for ages."

"Can we open our stockings yet?"

"Course not, silly, it's still tonight. Father Christmas hasn't even been here yet. You've only been sleeping a little while."

"Bother! What's the time?" Penny crawled to the end of the bed and felt the long woollen stocking of Dad's, which she had fastened there earlier. It hung limp and empty.

"Janet hasn't even come to bed yet. Ssh!" Patty whispered. "There's someone coming."

The floor boards were creaking on the landing, but it did not sound like ordinary footfalls. The twins lay silent.

"I don't hear anyone," whispered Penny. "Do you think it's Father Christmas?" Although they both knew perfectly well that it was Mother and Dad who filled their stockings, the lingering belief in that dear, benevolent, white-bearded person was something they hated to give up.

Suddenly, a deep growl sounded at the crack of the door, then a roar, and something on four feet came galloping into the room. Patty and Penny instantly dived under the bedclothes, clutching the bolster. With hearts thumping, they waited for the "thing" to pounce.

In a minute it felt as though a ten-footed cat were jumping all over them, pinching and tickling through the blankets. They screamed for mercy. "What are two kids doing talking at this hour of the night?" a gruff voice said. "If they don't go to sleep in five minutes Father Christmas won't be able to come down the chimney. He's just rattling over the roofs now."

Both girls threw back the bedclothes and sat up.

"Oh Jim, you scared us, you old tease," they giggled.

"Of course! I meant to! But really truly, I've been sent to tell you to shut up. You'd jolly well better get to sleep —or else!"

Giving them each a pretend spank, he disappeared.

"Leave the door ajar," they called after him. The narrow crack of light was friendly in the darkness.

In ten minutes they really were asleep.

Somehow, *this* night always seemed the longest of all the year. At an early hour Patty awoke. It was pitch dark. She stretched out her legs as far as she could, then wiggled further down the bed till her toe touched something, a firm object. Trembling with excitement, she wiggled back again, and sat up, staring into the darkness. Her eyes began to see the outline of objects. Yes, no doubt about it! Their stockings were fat, with things sticking out of the top. Father Christmas *had* been! It was morning!

She hugged herself in rapture. How could she endure such joy till her twin woke up!

Suddenly her ear caught the sound of music, far away— a trumpet, horn and drum, and voices singing. Yes, that was

"Once in Royal David's City." Who could be out there singing, so early in the darkness?

Patty remembered. It must be the Salvation Army, who always played through the little town on Christmas morning, but she only remembered once before being awake to hear it. Now she lay listening, enchanted, with little shivers of excitement running down her spine. Should she wake Penny to hear it, too? Yet, for this moment, she was enjoying the secretness of hearing the music alone. She knew some people thought the Army band music raucous, but to Patty, in that moment of excited anticipation, not even the heavenly choir itself could have sounded more thrilling.

> *"Peace on earth, and mercy mild . . .*
> *Hark the herald angels sing,*
> *Glory to the new-born King."*

Sometime later Patty felt her arm being tugged.

"What's the matter?" she said sleepily.

"Aren't you *ever* going to wake up?" complained Penny. "I've been waiting for you to, for ages. Father Christmas has been and I'm sure it must be half-past six. Let's get Janet to light the candle."

Instantly Patty was wide awake. She sat up.

"*I* was awake a *long* time ago," she declared.

"I don't believe it."

"Yes I was. I heard the music too!" Patty forgot she had meant to keep that a secret.

"What music? You might have waked me."

63

"There's something here *on* the bed, as well as in our stockings," whispered Patty loudly, changing the subject.

"For goodness' sake, be quiet, you two. *I* want to sleep." Janet's voice came from the single bed.

"Oh, *please* light the candle," the twins chimed together. "It must be past six o'clock. *Do* look at the time."

"It's only a little after half-past five. I heard the town clock strike," said Janet firmly.

"How do you know it wasn't half-past six?" came the twins' quick reply.

"Because I struck a match and looked. Now dry up! I'll let you know when it's time."

"Grumpy old thing," muttered the twins under the bed-clothes. "How *can* she want to sleep on Christmas morning? She must be getting dreadfully old."

"Yes, just like old Nanny."

"Maybe she'll grow fat like that and wear corsets." The thought of their pretty sister looking like old Nanny sent the twins into fits of giggles and they had to bury their faces in their pillows to smother the sound.

After what seemed an eternity, they heard Janet striking matches. They sat bolt upright.

"Two minutes to go," said Janet, in a more cheerful voice. "But you could start putting on your dressing gowns. Patty, you shut the window, and Penny, bring me the other candle." She lit it from her own. "Careful now, put it down on the chest of drawers."

Hands trembling with excitement, Penny obeyed. Janet counted ten, slowly.

"Now! Happy Christmas! But don't make too much noise!" she warned, and snuggled down under her bedclothes.

In a frenzy of joy the twins dived to the end of the big bed.

Now that this glorious moment had arrived, they spun it out as long as possible. The bulging stockings were hugged, squeezed and felt. The larger packages on the foot of the bed were guessed at. Then one by one everything was undone. Almost unbearable was the thrill of diving a hand into the dark woolly interior of the stocking leg, not knowing what might appear—doll's furniture, a skipping rope, knitted gloves, miniature toys, Tom Thumb books, gorgeous colored crayons, trinkets, a sumptuous pencil set. Every newfound treasure brought further shouts of joy.

Sleep for Janet was quite out of the question now. After awhile she decided to give up the attempt altogether. From under her pillow she produced a well-wrapped bar of cream-filled chocolate (her favorite private indulgence). Breaking off two sections she handed one to each twin.

"Here's something to keep you going, kidlets," she said, munching contentedly, and reaching for her book.

"For *us?* To eat *now*, before breakfast?" beamed Penny and Patty in amazement. Christmas certainly was wonderful!

Always there were several small square envelopes in their stockings containing shiny florins or half crowns, from the aunts and uncles. These Janet took charge of immediately, lest they be lost in the welter of tissue and brown paper. Lastly, there was an orange and a hard green apple in each toe.

Just as the twins always saved the icing on their cake till last, so the final largest parcel for each, on which they recognized Daddy's neat printing, was the last to be opened.

Dared they believe it was what they hoped for? The shape of each long box suggested it.

"It *is!*" they both shouted, as each lifted lid revealed the most beautiful doll either girl had ever hoped to own. Not only did the dolls have silky curled hair and long lashes over their sleeping eyes, but arms and legs that could move at every joint and the daintiest hands, with separate fingers.

Patty thought her heart would burst with joy as she gently lifted this dainty new child and hugged her. "Mine has blue eyes! *Such* beautiful eyes."

"Mine has brown," responded Penny, equally delighted. "I *love* brown eyes—like my boy doll. What shall we christen them?"

A long discussion ensued, without any final decisions, with Janet making helpful, but unaccepted suggestions. Even she admitted how pretty the dolls were and offered to help make them some clothes. At the moment they wore only the usual chemise, socks and shoes. But in addition there was a white fur cap and muff for each. When the twins learned later that their Mother had made these her-self from a white rabbit skin, their admiration knew no bounds.

A visit to Mother and Dad's room, to show them their new children, was the next thing to do, and to show every-one they met—Maggie taking cans of hot water to visitors' rooms; Aunt Milly on her way downstairs; and Geoff, trying out a new model railway coach on the landing. A chewed looking piece of string hung from his mouth.

"Thanks for the sugar mice, you kids. They were jolly good."

"Have you eaten them *all?*" The twins were horrified.

"Oh," said Penny suddenly. "We *forgot* to say thank you to Aunt Milly for the money."

They looked at each other in consternation.

Unexpected Guests

Breakfast was a happy, haphazard meal, at which the grownups opened their gifts and exclaimed over such dull things (to the twins' minds) as umbrellas, cuff links, soap, or leather-bound books with no pictures in them. Granny had breakfast quietly in her room. Penny and Patty munched scrambled eggs on buttered toast and drank cocoa. They tried to remember to thank the right people, and enjoyed being thanked and praised for their own hand-made gifts. It was fun receiving these attentions, though the endless question, "which of you is which?" became boring.

To their surprise, when the postman arrived there was a parcel for each of them from Aunt Margery up in the North.

"A book!" they said to each other, feeling the hard corners.

"Better wait till you've finished eating," reminded Mother. They hurried to finish their meal.

Penny's proved to be *Peter Pan* with beautiful soft misty pictures by Arthur Rackham. Patty's book was Hans Christian Andersen's *Fairy Tales*, a fat book with *lots* of pictures. She sighed happily, and went into raptures over the colored ones.

"One day, *I'll* draw pictures like this," she said to herself. Christmas was getting lovelier every moment.

When everyone assembled in the drawing room for family prayers, Granny was already seated in her special armchair, with a little table before her on which Daddy placed the big Bible. Chairs were ranged all round the room for everyone. The twins squeezed, pushing and whispering, into a low armchair together, with a warning look from

Mother. Three chairs near the door stood empty, for the two maids and the cook who, in answer to Geoff's tattoo on the big brass gong in the hall, came rustling upstairs in their starched morning aprons and cotton dresses, and took

their places modestly, hands folded in their laps. Penny caught Maggie's eye and grinned. Mrs. Johnson, the cook, looked like a mountain and just as imperturbable. Polly, the young housemaid, was so shy she kept her eyes on the carpet all the time.

Granny's soft voice began to read from the Gospel of Luke. "And it came to pass, in those days, that there went out a decree from Caesar Augustus, that all the world should be taxed. . . ."

As she listened, Patty could see it all happening so clearly, the village street, the stable (just like the one where Dobbin was, but with real animals), the tired mother and father, the shepherds coming down from the hills, and the wonder of the baby.

As the reading ended, and they all turned around to kneel, Patty whispered in Penny's ear, "I've decided to call mine Mary."

"Mine's going to be Josephine," whispered back Penny triumphantly.

While Granny prayed, Patty wondered about the shepherds. Did they really bring gifts as some of the old pictures and stories said? Of course the kings did. They were rich. She wondered if *she* could have parted with a newborn lamb, or her new doll. What *would* she have brought?

After a hymn had been sung and a blessing pronounced, Granny asked them all to wait. She had something to tell them.

"I just heard this morning that a missionary and his wife arrived unexpectedly in our town last night from China.

Our own minister is kindly putting them up for a few nights, but has asked if I would give them hospitality for today.

"We are a big party already, I know," Granny went on, looking a little anxiously toward Cook and Aunt Milly, "but I sent word that of course we would be delighted to make room for three more. They have a child, I understand, about your age, children," and she looked toward the twins. "You will take special charge of the boy or girl, won't you? No doubt you can find something nice among your new gifts to help make this child's Christmas happy. Anyway, I'm sure we will all do our part to show these strangers the warmth of an English Christmas, which they have not had for so long."

The twins nodded soberly at Granny, then exchanged glances with each other. Now all began to disperse, giving their warm approval. Patty felt a twinge of anguish, as if clouds were already gathering over this golden morning. Why must there be strangers, foreigners, coming in? It was fun to be special—just Geoff, Penny and herself the only young children among all the grownups. Give away? How could she *give* a present that she had barely got for her own? And to someone she didn't even know? There hadn't been time to even begin to enjoy everything yet. What ever would they do?

Mother found the twins in an anxious huddle over this problem five minutes later.

"In Sunday school they say you should always give your best, the thing that means most to you. Mummy, does that really mean we've got to give our new dolls?" Penny asked mournfully. "And we've *just* decided on their names."

"I don't *think* Granny meant that," answered their mother, "besides, I'm quite sure I heard Uncle Gerald say the child is a boy, so he's probably not interested in dolls."

"Oh I *hope* it's a boy," said Patty fervently.

"Is he Chinese? Will his eyes go like this?" And Penny dragged the ends of her eyelids up into slits. Patty giggled in spite of herself.

"Don't do that!" Mother's voice was quite sharp. "No, they are English, as you are. But sometimes children born and brought up in a foreign country look a little different, when they are young. I want to see you being as kind and friendly as possible. It will be rather frightening for the little chap, coming into a big household like this. Now, what are you each going to choose for a gift?"

There was a long and painful silence while the girls surveyed their little pile of treasures and wrestled with their consciences. At the moment it seemed agony to part with anything, yet they did really want to be unselfish.

Finally Penny pulled a square flat box from her pile and said, "Do you think my plasticine set would be nice? Either a boy *or* girl could use it."

Patty knew by the moist look in her sister's eyes that this was a wrench. The plasticine set was something she had been specially thrilled with.

"Then I'll give my diamond-topped pencils," she announced in a rush, lest her mind should change as she spoke. She held up the box of six assorted pencils with shiny metal caps on each of which glittered a lovely piece of colored glass. They were highly prized at school. Patty had gloated over the thought of how her friends would covet them.

"Capital," said Mother. "Those are presents that any child will enjoy, I'm sure. Granny will be pleased. It's time to be getting ready for church. We shall be meeting this new family there. Don't dawdle now," and Mother went down to her room.

"I do *hope* church won't be too long today. It's going to

be so difficult to sit still on those hard pews when there's our new dolls and so *much* to play with here." Patty sighed as she smoothed some tissue paper to wrap the precious pencils in.

"Yes, I know," agreed Penny. "But there's sure to be nice Christmas hymns, and I love feeling how the sound of the organ makes my back tingle, don't you?"

They each slipped a tiny stocking present in their pockets, to secretly feel and peep at during the service. Penny's was a doll's house flatiron. Patty picked a little red leather notebook, with a pencil attached, which Jim had given her.

"But you can't draw in church!" reproved her sister.

"Can't I?" Patty grinned wickedly.

It was a typical damp mild Christmas morning as the family sallied forth, to the accompaniment of church bells echoing through the old town. Sitting next to Dad, Patty dared not produce her notebook, but the service did not seem long at all; there were lots of hymns they knew, the favorite Bible story which Granny had read, and some interesting ladies' hats to observe.

"That must be *them*," whispered Penny, nudging her sister, when, an hour later, they all filed out of church. Granny and Uncle Gerald were talking to a tall man and his pale wife, while beside them stood a little boy. He was thin and pale, too, and looked as though none of his clothes belonged to him.

"It *is* a boy." Patty sighed with relief. "And they *aren't* Chinese."

"But he doesn't look very exciting," responded Penny.

"Maybe we shan't have to bother about him too much after all."

"We'll have to do something though, and Mum said we mustn't take him to see all our presents; that would be showing off."

"Just think, we probably shan't be able to play with Mary and Josephine *all* the rest of today," grumbled Patty. "Bother! I wish he hadn't come."

Fortunately these uncharitable comments were put to a stop when Uncle Gerald called them over to meet the newcomers, Mr. and Mrs. Newman and their son, Richard.

(A big surprise awaited them.)

After the first formal introduction to Richard, progress was almost at a standstill. He *was* shy. He spoke only in monosyllables. All they learned during the walk back to Granny's was that he was a half year younger than they, although, in a way, he seemed older, that he was often called Rick, that he liked school in China, and had never seen a plum pudding.

He accepted the girls' proffered gifts solemnly, with a little bow, but they could not tell whether he was really pleased with them or not.

What a waste, Penny was thinking to herself, wondering if he really appreciated their self-sacrifice.

Richard Newman took the presents to show his parents, while Patty and Penny went upstairs to change.

Christmas dinner at 1:30, the second high point of the

day, was a gala affair. The table glittered with silver and glass, ornaments and gay Christmas decorations on the white damask cloth. Everyone wore party clothes.

In one way it was rather an ordeal to the twins. Food was rarely the *most* interesting thing in life to them and now excitement reduced their appetites still further.

"I'm always afraid I won't be able to eat all that's on my plate," admitted Patty, as she pulled on her best white socks. To leave food was considered a shameful lack of manners.

"Or that I'll forget what it is I have to say to my neighbor."

"Yes, I know. I always dread the Loving Cup," agreed her sister.

At Granny's, it was a long-honored custom to pass round a loving cup to the guests at table on this special day. A large, two-handled silver cup, about twelve inches high, filled with some delectable drink was placed at the head of the table, between the second and third courses. With gracious ceremony, beginning with Granny, each person in turn would rise from his seat and turn to his left hand neighbor, who had also risen, and address him solemnly.

"I drink to thee, friend, as my friend has drunk to me." Then the speaker took a sip from the cup, and wiping it, passed it to his neighbor with the words, "Do thou drink to thy friend, as I have drunk to thee."

Somehow the solemnity of this was always awe-inspiring to the younger generation—they would get confused and the "thees" and "thous"—or the "drink" and "drunk" always got mixed up.

At this moment there was a bang on the door and in walked Geoff, dressed in only half his Eton suit, with collar in one hand and the stud and tie in the other. The jacket was under his arm.

"SOS! Mum, *can* you help me with this confounded thing?" he blurted out. "I *can't* get it to go right! Who invented the beastly things anyway?"

"Ssh," said Mother. "I'll see to it in just a minute."

"Here, I'll give you a hand," said Janet, who was in her petticoat, doing her hair.

"The only part I *really* like is dessert at the end," confessed Penny, ignoring the interruption. "Those lovely shiny crystalized fruits and the dates."

"*And* pulling the crackers!" prompted Patty, "especially when they have paper hats *and* whistles in them."

"Do you remember that American chap at our school?" Geoff broke in. "He used to call crackers 'snappers.' Wasn't that queer?"

"I don't think so," said Janet, still wrestling with the starched collar. "If you think of it, I suppose they snap just as much as they crack, really."

"It's that smell of gunpowder and a real *bang* that I like best," said Geoff.

"And to find something in the pudding!" added Penny. As Mother tied their pink satin hair ribbons she promised to see that they were given portions suitable in size and repeated with them the little Loving Cup speech.

"I'm sure Aunt Milly or Auntie Grace will help you out. Don't worry, darlings."

At last all of them were ready, looking their best. With the added poise that their new clothes gave them, Patty and Penny took their appointed places at the long dining table, each seated beside an attentive maiden aunt. But Richard Newman sat next to his mother. They watched as eagerly as everyone else, when Maggie, her face flushed, carried in the big serving dish, crowned with a dome-shaped silver dish cover, and placed it before Uncle Gerald.

Meanwhile, Polly placed a boiled ham in front of Dad, who was already sharpening his carving knife and cracking jokes with a nephew. The aroma of roast turkey had been filling the house for hours. Now the great moment had come!

There was a quiet pause, while Granny said grace.

Maggie reached over and lifted the dish cover with a flourish. (Had anyone noticed, the corners of her mouth were twitching violently.) There was a second of astonished silence, then a roar of laughter echoed to the ceiling. In the middle of the serving dish lay one tiny browned sausage, in a nest of parsley. Outside the dining room door, Mrs. Johnson's ample form was shaking like jelly, enjoying to the full the success of her little joke. Only as old a servant as she would have dared think of such a thing. Not even Aunt Milly had been forewarned! It was a complete success!

Midst the merriment, Uncle Gerald flourished his knife and fork over this tiny object and asked, "Heads or tails, Geoffrey?"

By the look on Geoff's face, it was plain that he had not entirely understood the joke. Was this *really* all there was going to be for Christmas dinner?

Before he had time to answer, in came Mrs. Johnson bearing an even bigger dish, with a still bigger dish cover, which, next minute, revealed the largest roast turkey Geoff had ever seen. It was deep golden brown and surrounded by a whole army of shiny brown sausages. He beamed with satisfaction. Polly now appeared, carrying in each hand dishes piled with snowy mashed potatoes, and Brussels sprouts. Rich brown gravy was served from a silver vessel resembling a curled shell. The feast could begin!

Dinner was necessarily a lengthy affair. No one hurried. In spite of his slender appearance, the twins noticed how well Richard applied himself to his dinner, finishing every scrap, and even accepting a second helping, as did many others.

"He's probably never had such a dinner before, poor little chap," whispered Aunt Milly.

Next came the great black shiny plum pudding, topped with a sprig of holly. There was custard sauce to pour on top and there were little mince pies too, for those who wished.

Patty loved the custard, but she only forced herself to eat some pudding to see if she could find a charm in her slice. Penny, with a crow of delight, found the tiny silver wishbone in hers. Jim, with plenty of teasing from uncles and cousins, had discovered the ring and a threepenny bit!

"You'll need it," laughed Janet. She was looking radiant in her new green silk dress, and thoroughly enjoying the chaffing of an older boy cousin. Rick got the sixpence!

"Real money you can spend," they told him.

Patty munched on, downheartedly. She felt about with her spoon—nothing! She was sure of it. Her disappointment was intense.

"Are you *sure?*" asked a young uncle beside her. "I believe you dropped a piece on the floor."

Patty *knew* she hadn't spilled, she'd tried to be so careful, but she leaned down to look, all the same. "No, I didn't," she said mournfully.

Then, wonder of wonders, the next time she raised her spoon, something on her plate glinted. "Oh joy!" She sucked the object clean. "The little silver pig!"

"For good luck!" Aunt Milly said. "And you need not eat any more if you don't want to."

Patty's happiness was complete and she felt absolutely full. Even the ordeal of the Loving Cup which came next wouldn't be so bad now. She watched and listened to the others with a fluttering heart. Jim got all mixed up and drank to himself by mistake, to everyone's amusement, but he didn't seem to mind.

To Penny's great relief, Auntie Grace suggested that all she need say would be "I drink to thee." So when it came Patty's turn, she did the same to Aunt Milly. That was wonderful! Now she was ready for the best part of all—pulling the crackers—everyone wearing paper hats (yes,

and some with whistles or trinkets too)—cracking nuts—
and peeling tangerines! And even Patty found room for
a lovely sticky crystalized apricot, one chocolate and two
grapes. After which fingers were elegantly dipped in her
cut glass finger bowl and the banquet came to an end.

Surprises

W$_{\text{HILE}}$ some of the grownups retired to rest, others chatted or snoozed in the drawing room. Jim and the other cousins became engrossed in Geoff's model railway trains. Janet was closeted in the seclusion of the blue room with an older girl cousin and her new manicure set. Dad was deep in conversation with Richard's father.

The twins naturally joined forces and invited Rick to play with them. Now he seemed a different person. He suggested that they open the plasticine box and make things. That was decent of him, Penny thought. It gave her and Patty a chance to enjoy it too. She went in search of Aunt Milly to beg some sheets of newspaper to work on. They spread their things in the back passage and went to work.

Soon Rick's nimble fingers were busy.

"I say! You're good at making things, aren't you?" The twins gazed in admiration as, one after another, small animals and objects were fashioned from the lumps of sticky pink and grey stuff. Patty, who had always thought herself rather good at this, felt slow and clumsy by comparison.

"Yours look so real! How do you get the legs to stay on so well?" she asked.

"Just pinch them out of the lump—like this!" It looked so easy the way Rick did it.

Before long, the rolls of plasticine had all been transformed into a sizeable menagerie, complete with trainers, drivers and on-lookers. Penny made some children.

"It seems too bad to squash them all up into the box again. Let's save them to show the others." They decided to find a bigger box so that Rick could take the menagerie home intact.

"Now what shall we do?"

"What about using the newspaper?" suggested Rick.

"How?"

"Folding," he replied simply. "A friend of my father's showed me." Deftly he tore off a square of newspaper, and folded it over, then again, then diagonally. Folding and twisting, turning and folding, while the twins watched the paper wad grow smaller and thicker. Then, with a little tug here, a flick there, suddenly there appeared a paper bird, complete with beak and tail.

"Why, its wings can even flap!" they exclaimed. As Rick carefully manipulated the tail, the head and wings moved, too.

"I say! You *are* clever! I'm sure we could never do that. It must take a long time to learn. Do you know some more folding things?"

Rick did, and tore off more paper.

"I bet you are good at drawing, too," said Patty, a little anxiously. She hoped she might have a chance to show off a little in this field herself. She wished she'd brought that best picture with her. Rick might have been impressed.

"Yes, I like drawing," answered Rick. "But in China they paint mostly. They both write and draw with brushes. It will be fun to use pens and pencils more, especially those beautiful diamond-topped ones," he added, smiling at Patty.

"Of course they aren't *real* jewels, you know," said Patty truthfully. "But at our school we think they're awfully special."

At that moment Mother discovered them.

"*Here* you children are! I thought you were all in the garden. It's high time you got some fresh air. Playing with plasticine with *no* pinafores on?" She frowned at the twins momentarily, but fortunately, seeing no visible smears on the new dresses, she refrained from further rebuke.

"Clear up now. Then run along, twins, and put your coats and hats on. Daddy and the others are going for a walk. You would like to join them, wouldn't you, Richard?"

Rick nodded. Picking up the plasticine box and lid and a folded newspaper all covered with small models, he went in search of his parents.

"Look what Rick made, Mummy! Isn't he clever?" chimed the girls, and they displayed the paper bird. Then they raced upstairs. The older girls, now resplendent with highly polished fingernails, were just about to leave the room.

"Coming for a walk with Dad and the others?" asked Janet.

"Yes, but we *can't* go out without taking our dolls, can we?" They looked at each other. "They need fresh air, too."

"Boys so often think dolls are silly."

"And yet Rick seems different somehow."

"Oh, I should take them, and never mind what boys say," put in Janet. "But they look a bit indecent the way they are. You'd better wrap them up more or they might catch cold too." She turned to open a drawer.

"Look, take this wool scarf of mine for one of them, and the other can have this big cotton square." She paused.

"But be *very* careful of them, mind. *Don't* let them trail in the mud. And remember to give them back."

"That's ripping of you! Thanks ever so much!" The twins were thrilled with this generous offer.

They agreed to risk it. With a woolly scarf and kerchief wound round each, to cover their scanty attire, the dolls, resplendent in their fur caps and muffs, were brought down and introduced to Rick.

He looked at them respectfully, admiring their eyes and eyelashes, also the delicate hands and the way the wrist joints worked.

During the walk they told him how they had decided on the names. Rick approved. He even offered to be godfather to them, if they liked. This pleased and flattered the twins enormously.

The third climax of this day was now approaching. After tea, for which, understandably, no one was very hungry, in spite of the handsomely iced cake decorated with pink sugar and candles, it was time to prepare for the Christmas play.

Jim and the other big cousins got busy arranging chairs in rows, and fetching screens and needed properties from the kitchen. Up in the blue room, Geoff, Penny and Patty struggled into their costumes with Mother's help and numerous admonitions.

"What'll I do if I forget?" asked Penny anxiously.

"I've got a funny feeling in my middle," added Patty.

"Nonsense! You'll do it perfectly all right," was their

Mother's encouraging reply. "And anyway, I'll be near the door, to prompt you if need be."

"By Jove, if anyone pulls my hair it'll come right off. I know it will!" This was Geoff's private worry.

However, once they got started, all was well, although such a burst of laughter and clapping greeted the first appearance of Tweedledum and Tweedledee after Jim removed the stage screen, that Patty nearly lost her head and her first lines.

The audience responded wonderfully and laughed in all the right places as well as in a few wrong ones. Rick sat on the edge of a stool, wrapped in solemn attention.

On the final exit Patty lost her way, because Granny's saucepan that she was wearing was so much bigger than the one she had used for rehearsals. She bumped into the door post. Penny, completely enveloped by the smallest coal scuttle available, tripped on her own eiderdown and crashed into Patty. There was an exchange of muffled but very unladylike retorts. The next minute there were sounds of a large metal object going bong! bong! plonkity, bong! down the front stairs.

"Goodness, gracious!" And Mother made a hasty exit, too, while "Alice" with complete calm, but "her" wig slightly askew, spoke the closing lines.

The whole thing, however, was judged a great success, and Granny praised them all warmly for their efforts. Later, re-dressed in their velveteen frocks, Penny and Patty each performed on their instruments, accompanied by Janet. In spite of all her efforts to feel calm, Patty's hands shook, her bow *would* wobble, and her fingers were sticky with nervousness. Penny's cello piece sounded considerably better, she knew. However, when the ordeal was over, she packed her fiddle into its case, then squeezed on to the couch next to Aunt Milly.

"Is it time to play charades, now?" she asked.

"Not yet. First I think we have someone rather important coming to see us," her aunt replied.

"Not *more* visitors? Tonight?"

The twins were conscious of a curious air of mystery and expectancy in the room.

The tall screen had been placed across the room again, as it had been for their play. Now Uncle Gerald came forward.

"Friends! And assembled guests!" he said, in a very professional sort of voice. "I am happy to tell you that we have yet another treat this evening. We are about to be honored with a visit from a very special personage, who, by the way, only reached our shores a few hours ago. May I present, none other, than His Royal Highness—The Dwarf!"

Everyone gasped! Someone outside the door beat a tattoo with tin lids, the screen was removed and there sat the most amazing little man. He was about as wide as he was high. He sat on a table that was covered with a long red cloth, and he was bowing and smiling to the assembled company.

His head seemed a normal size, with a great snowy beard (just like Grandpa's, in his portrait, thought Patty), but his body was very short. The Dwarf wore a curious assortment of clothes, including a red fez on his head, a richly embroidered stole, beads, bracelets, a wedding ring, earrings, and red turkish leather slippers on his feet, which stuck straight out in front of him.

Richard and the twins wiggled with excitement and studied him in mystified awe.

"Yoou must ixcusse me, laydees and jenteelmen," the Dwarf was saying, in rather a foreign accent, "eef I do not ri-i-ase to gree-e-t you, but I am a leetle ti-ured after my lo-o-ong journey."

Then he went on to tell them something about his travels. He asked and answered numerous questions. He spotted Rick and invited him to come and shake hands with him, which Rick did, as if in a dream. Then the Dwarf reached, with much fumbling, into the folds of his garments and produced a silver threepenny bit ("like the one Jim got in the pudding," whispered Penny).

"To remember me by," said the Dwarf graciously, folding his hands again and nodding sagely at Rick.

Where was Jim, anyway, wondered Penny suddenly. She glanced quickly round the room. And Daddy, too? Perhaps they were seeing to the Dwarf's carriage? She *hoped* they wouldn't miss meeting *him*.

Next, Patty plucked up courage to offer the Dwarf a chocolate, at someone's suggestion. He accepted, but seemed to have some difficulty getting it into his mouth. He fumbled and dropped the first, so Patty offered him a second. This one found its destination. Patty noticed the ring he wore was similar to Daddy's.

In a moment of mischievousness Geoff bobbed up to him and tweaked his beard. The Dwarf was furious. He drummed his heels on the table and shouted, "Off with his head!" Geoff didn't really seem to mind.

However, soon mollified by soothing remarks and compliments from Uncle Gerald, His Highness agreed to sing a little song before his departure.

He rocked to and fro, wagging his toes and clapping his hands and singing, "Rule, Britannia." As everyone joined in the chorus, Uncle Gerald drew the screen across, applause broke out and someone started up the musical box.

"Can we see him go?" the twins clamored excitedly.

"No, he doesn't like being watched," was the firm reply and Uncle Gerald effectually blocked their way. "But you could run to the window and look behind the curtain. You *might* catch a glimpse of him getting into his carriage."

Rick and the girls pressed their noses against the cold glass and looked down on to the deserted lamp-lit pavements. Who was the Dwarf really? How far did he come? Where was he going back to? They kept wondering. Then, far up the street could be heard a single retreating horse and carriage, clip, clop, clip, clop.

"We must have *missed* him," they said to each other, in puzzled surprise.

"Coo! He must have got down to the front door jolly fast," observed Rick. He stood for a minute, studying his threepenny bit.

"I *believe* I guess," he began.

"Guess what?" asked the twins.

"Come on, everybody. Who's ready to play charades?" called Uncle Gerald.

"*We* are!" With one bound Patty and Penny were at his side.

Long past their usual bedtime, after farewells and good nights had been said, Mother shepherded the twins upstairs, yawning their heads off as they went.

"No baths tonight," she was saying. "Just brush your teeth, sponge your faces, and pop into bed as fast as you can. It's been a long day."

"I can't even remember when it began. But it's been the *loveliest* Christmas day we've ever had," chimed two sleepy voices.

"Look, they've stayed awake for you, too," said Mother,

as they entered the blue room. Patty and Penny ran toward the bed, where the two new dolls sat, propped against the pillow, each holding a tiny teddy bear.

"You darlings! I hope you didn't think we'd forgotten you." They hugged and kissed them.

"But you *might* have been frightened by the Dwarf," whispered Patty into Mary's ear. "Will the Dwarf come again next year, do you think, Mummy? Wasn't he funny?"

"And will Rick come, too?" asked Penny pulling her nightie over her head. "I *do* hope so!"

"He's the nicest boy we've ever met," they agreed. "And he *said* he'd write!"

"I'm so glad, darlings," said Mother, as she hung up the new dresses. "But there's a whole year to wait till next Christmas. We'll see. Now, night-night."

Before she reached the door, they were asleep.

ǝ CHAPTER ELEVEN

A WINTER PICNIC

THE wonderful thing about the morning after Christmas was to wake up and find it *had* been real after all! Here were all the pristine treasures, to prove it. Real, tangible, still intact, ready to be enjoyed all over again.

"The main difference is," observed Penny, "now we *know* what we've got. Yesterday we were only discovering."

There was time for a good half hour of play in bed before having to get up.

Janet was absorbed in her book.

This was Boxing Day, that nice leisurely *extra* holiday that followed Christmas; the day when all the cooks and maids and shopkeepers and other workers had their day off. It was like an extra Saturday, *after* a Sunday.

In comfortable shabby old clothes, everyone began preparing for this day's particular event, which was under

95

Dad's direction. As well as a nature lover, he was also a keen woodsman. Every Boxing Day he loved to lead a family expedition where there was some ill-fated or mis-shapen tree that needed felling, either on his own, or some of the family's land. This year, it was to be a lightning-struck pine on Aunt Grace's farm, about four miles away. That sounded exciting.

"Will Rick be coming, too?" asked Penny and Patty eagerly.

"No, I'm afraid not, dears. He and his parents have to go on to London today," was Aunt Milly's reply. She went to the kitchen, where she and mother and the other aunts began cutting piles of sandwiches and preparing the picnic lunch.

The twins ran in and begged a tiny potato or carrot to take out to Dobbin. Two lumps of sugar were secured, too. Inside the stable they found Uncle Gerald and Jim, who were looking the old rocking horse over.

"It wouldn't take much to fix him up," Jim was saying. "I believe Dad and I could do it ourselves."

"Bringing Dobbin a bite?" said their uncle, when he saw the girls. "He'll certainly be glad of a little attention. He must be pretty lonely these days." And he and Jim departed.

"What a pity Rick didn't see Dobbin," said Penny, as she tried to make a piece of carrot stay between the horse's teeth.

"But it wouldn't have been so much good, since we can't ride him," replied Patty, alternately sucking one end of her lump of sugar and offering the other half to Dobbin, while she stroked the smooth wooden neck.

In half an hour, Dad, Jim, Janet, Geoff, Uncle Gerald, Aunt Milly, Aunt Grace, two older cousins, Penny and Patty, as well as three other assorted aunts and uncles, all boarded the bus in the village square. They were laden with two picnic baskets, rucksacks, axes, hatchets, wedges, and a crosscut saw. Mother decided to have a quiet day at home with Granny.

As the bus halted near the railway station, Penny and Patty caught a glimpse of passengers waiting for a train. Suddenly they spied Rick and his parents.

"There's Rick. Look!" And they pounded their woollen fists on the bus window. "Rick! Rick!"

He could not have heard them, but something made him look that way. He saw them just in time. His solemn little face lit up, and happy wavings of recognition and farewell were exchanged, before the bus resumed its journey, lurching and bumping over the countryside. It stopped frequently to deposit or pick up passengers.

It was a fine day, colder and clearer than yesterday. Everyone seemed in holiday mood. Now the bus was grinding its way up a long hill. Slower and slower it went, the sound of the gears getting rougher and deeper. Suddenly it lurched, backfired, stopped, started again spasmodically once or twice, then stopped altogether. Conversation broke out, the driver jumped from his seat and peered inside the bonnet and started tinkering. The conductor got out to see if he could help. Soon they were joined by Jim, Geoff, and any number of other boys and men. But the bus still stood there, a lifeless thing.

"What ever will happen to us all?" asked Penny.

Just then the driver put his head into the bus and asked if anyone had a good length of strong string. Not surprisingly, Dad was the one who could produce it. He always seemed prepared for any emergency.

The driver made some needed repair to the bus engine, and cranked her up. The engine jangled to life. Then all climbed back into their seats and off they went again. "Hurrah!" the passengers cheered.

At last the family alighted near Auntie Grace's farm. While the men went off to plan the tree felling, Janet, another aunt and the twins helped Auntie Grace fetch cups and kettles and the coffee pot from her cottage, and carry them to the picnic site, where the fire would be built. When they got to the spinney, Dad and Uncle Gerald had already started work with their axes.

Patty and Penny danced round the fringes of activity, picking up chips and helping to collect dry sticks for the fire. Because the tree grew close to another good one, with several others near, it needed careful judgment to bring it down in exactly the right spot. Jim climbed up it like a monkey and attached a rope according to Dad's directions.

At the appointed time, when the tree seemed to have little left to stand on, Dad called most of those present to take their places at the rope, to guide the tree's fall in the right direction. Patty and Penny usually watched, half scared, half excited. There was not the slightest possibility of anyone getting hurt with Dad's careful planning.

"But does it hurt the tree?" they always wondered.

One more judicious axe cut, then Dad stepped back and gave the trunk a push. It quivered.

"Pull," shouted Dad.

The tree rocked, then slowly, slowly it started its sweep toward the earth. Like a tug-of-war the others pulled on the rope, overcoming the tree's resistance.

"Let her go!" called Dad.

There was a thud. The earth shook, and everyone cheered. "Just the right spot," Dad was saying. But the twins looked on with moist eyes.

"Poor tree," murmured Penny. "I don't think it really wanted to go."

While the kettle came to a boil, everyone went to work with hatchets, lopping off branches, trimming, hacking merrily. When the coffee was made Dad halted the work.

"Time for grub," he called cheerily. "My word, I bet you can all do with some, too. You've earned it. Good work, everyone!"

"I'm *famished*, Dad," owned Geoff.

Never did cold turkey sandwiches or sausage rolls taste better. Even the twins ate hungrily. There were cold mince pies, biscuits, squares of nut chocolate and apples for a second course. Patty and Penny had "milk with a dash" to drink, and warmed their hands and feet by the crackling fire.

After lunch, a really big bonfire was organized, to tidy up the debris of useless branches. While work went on with the big crosscut saw, reducing the trunk to convenient lengths, many of the party were kept busy feeding the bonfire. The twins were set to fill the empty picnic baskets with chips for Auntie Grace's hearth. However, tiring of this after awhile, they wandered off for a little exploring.

"What a pity Rick isn't here. He'd have liked this, I expect," said Patty, as they left the spinney to follow a path by the hedge. Thrushes and blackbirds chuckled and fluttered in and out of the bare branches, eating the haws and other berries.

"Look, there's a bird's nest," said Penny excitedly.

"Only an *old* one, silly," replied Patty disdainfully.

"I know, but there's someone in it all the same. Wait!"

They stood still, staring. Sure enough, as they gazed, two

round ears appeared, and two beady black eyes looked at them over the rim of the nest, nose and whiskers twitching. The tip of a long tail hung over the rim of sticks and ragged moss. Then it disappeared.

The girls were so excited with their find that they raced back to tell Daddy.

"Come and see!" they urged.

He left his axe and wedges and came right away. They were just in time to see the little creature returning to the nest, with a large red berry in his mouth.

"Good for you, Penny. I'm glad you spotted that. You were using your eyes!" Dad praised. "Yes, that's a long-tailed field mouse. He's evidently using that old nest for his winter larder. He knows that no bird will be needing it. Now, come back with me. I've got something to show *you!*"

The twins skipped along expectantly.

Near the hedge, where the grass was long and tangled, Daddy indicated a ball-shaped mound, partly hidden by roots.

"Oh," said Penny, unimpressed. "It's just an old lump of dried grass."

"No, look carefully." And Dad gently rolled the lump from under cover, with the toe of his boot. By now Aunt Milly, Janet and several others joined them.

"What's going on?" they asked.

"See how the grasses are twisted round and round?" Dad was saying. They nodded. "Guess who's inside there?" Everyone guessed, but no one was right.

"That's a hedgehog's winter nest. He makes himself into a ball, then rolls round and round in the loose dry grass, till it mats all over his quills. He's right in the middle, inside there, sleeping."

"Really? Honestly?" Everyone was intrigued.

"How can he breathe? When will he wake up? How can he eat?" The twins were full of questions.

"I've never seen a *real* live hedgehog," said Penny.

Carefully Dad rolled the dormant hedgehog back into his hiding place.

"Let's look him up in my book when we get back, and I'll tell you all about him."

A tired happy crowd came home at dusk to a late high tea. Granny and Mother made a willing audience for all their adventures. Later, Dad regaled them all with an account of the private life of Mr. Hedgehog. Patty and Penny, with their dolls in their laps, subsided into a corner with their new books. When their mother ruled "early bed," the twins did not demur.

"I think I know *just* what that hedgehog feels like," said Penny, as she snuggled down in the big soft bed.

"Me, too," said Patty, and for a while they held hands across the bolster, whispering.

"I can't *believe* that Christmas Day was only yesterday, can you? It seems years ago!"

While strains of music—piano, an uncle's flute, Dad's violin, or vocal duets—floated up from the drawing room, Penny and Patty sleepily made elaborate plans for a *real* "day with the dolls" on the morrow.

CHAPTER TWELVE

An end and NEW BEGINNINGS

DECEMBER 27th dawned dark and drizzly. Several relatives left for home and Uncle Gerald had business at his office to see to.

By after breakfast, the rain was falling steadily.

"Bother!" said Penny, "now we can't take the dolls into the garden."

"But we planned to have a christening," said Patty.

"No we didn't! I don't *want* to pretend church this morning."

"Then I shan't play! I'd rather draw anyway."

An argument arose. They had both awakened feeling grumpy. The slightest disagreement was likely to set them off. When Janet discovered that Patty had borrowed the tiny brush from her new manicure set to brush her doll's hair with, the fat was certainly in the fire. Angry voices rose to a pitch, and Patty was practically in tears.

"*Take* your soppy old manicure thing—and I didn't hurt it anyway—so *there!*" And a small object went flying through the air just as Aunt Milly arrived at the door of the blue room.

She looked shocked. All three girls felt dreadfully ashamed. *What* would Mother have said?

After a long pause, broken only by sniffles from Patty and murmured attempts at apology by Janet, Aunt Milly said quietly, "Penelope, Granny would like to see you downstairs. You'll find her in the drawing room."

Instantly Penny's heart missed a beat. The broken bowl! Granny hadn't forgotten! Was she going to be punished after all? Perhaps she was going to have to mend it? Hesitantly, she smoothed her hair, straightened her stockings, and went toward the door, with only a furtive glance toward her twin.

"Patricia, you may put on your outdoor things and come with me. We are going to pay a call. Your mother has gone to see an old friend, and your father is busy this morning."

Aunty's tone was quiet but final. There could be no arguing. They left the room.

Janet, in a state of injured pride, decided to try putting her hair up, and then she'd go and spend some of her Christmas money on a pair of new gloves. She wished her cousin was still there.

When Penny opened the drawing room door she found Granny waiting for her. She was sitting on a small chair near the window, and had on a black satin apron over her grey gabardine dress. The doors of the glass cabinet were open, to Penny's surprise, and a low stool was standing near it.

"Come along, Penelope dear," said Granny, in her soft sweet voice, as Penny hesitated nervously near the door, holding on to the brass doorknob, after she had closed it.

"I have a little task that needs to be done here, and I thought it would be nice if you helped me with it. These shelves need sorting and rearranging. I don't know *when* they were last dusted thoroughly."

Penny gasped.

"You mean—you mean that *I'm* to help you dust your treasures, Granny?" she asked in amazement.

"Certainly," was the reply. "Your small hands can reach in there perfectly, and lift the things out. We'll begin on this side at the top. You can put each thing on this tray after you've dusted it."

Granny produced another apron and tied it round her granddaughter. Then Penny went to work, gingerly, scarcely believing the honor of the task that Granny had set her.

With a mixture of suppressed rebellion and curiosity Patty buttoned her coat, and struggled into the old galoshes that Aunt Milly insisted on her wearing. She couldn't bear the feeling of Mother not being there, to appeal to.

Her twin was in the drawing room with Granny. The door was closed. *What* were they doing? She longed to know, but would not bring herself to ask. She wished there had not been that squabble this morning. Feeling bereft and forlorn, she both longed for her twin, yet *didn't* want her there. Where were she and Aunt Milly going, anyway? The excursion, whatever it was, promised absolutely no excitement.

A large umbrella dripped over them both. Aunty carried a covered basket. She made several comments, to which Patty was unresponsive. However, it appeared that they were going to visit a Miss Perdy, Granny's old seamstress who used to work for her. A feeling of utter desolation enveloped Patty.

Finally, turning into a very narrow back street, Aunty stopped at a door, and rapped. Some grubby, poorly dressed children were sailing pieces of stick in the flowing gutter. They stared at Patty.

The door opened slowly, and there stood a thin, stooped, wrinkled old woman.

She must be *terribly* old, thought Patty, like the witches in fairy stories.

A toothless smile lightened the old face when Miss Perdy recognized Aunt Milly and she welcomed them in.

"Well, only for a brief visit," replied Aunty, adding, "and this is my niece, Miss Perdy; Patricia, one of Edward's twins, you remember." Patty hung back.

The strange stuffy smell beyond the door repelled her. She dreaded going into homes like this—if you could call it a home. Everything seemed crammed into just this tiny room. Taking a deep breath, Patty stepped over the threshold.

She sat on the very edge of a rather broken-down cane chair, letting her eyes rove over her surroundings. Aunt Milly unpacked the basket of cold turkey soup and other nourishing things, while she kept up a cheerful flow of conversation and inquiries.

Patty studied everything, from the astonishing creases on Miss Perdy's face, the old-fashioned brooch she wore, the neat but shabby black clothes, down to her carpet slippers; then the bed in the corner, the knick-knacks, family photos, dried flowers, a picture of King George V and Queen Mary with some holly stuck in the top, and a hundred and one other items in that chock-a-block room.

"How can anyone *live* here?" said Patty to herself

uncomfortably. Then her eyes were caught by a portrait on the wall behind her. She twisted around on her seat. The light in the room was dim, so the picture didn't show up too well. But she could see it was of a pretty young woman with a basket of flowers in her hand. It was a nice picture. Patty saw that the ring on the young woman's finger looked so real she could have touched it. How could anyone paint like that? It must be done with *real* gold! Miss Perdy became aware of Patty's absorption in the portrait.

"Would you like to go and look at it closer, dear?" she asked. "Your gran'mother gave me that. It was done by 'er sister. Oh, she painted somethin' wondiful, she did! It's me prize possession." And she started reminiscing.

Patty got up and gazed closely, her nose nearly on the canvas.

Why! It wasn't gold at all! Just a plain old bit of yellow-brown, with a big dab of white in the middle. What a delusion! Patty went back to her chair, yet from there the ring shone again as before, just as golden as ever. This astonishing discovery fascinated her. It obliterated everything around her. It filled her thoughts like a private revelation and she pondered it to herself all the way home, as she and Aunty walked back to Granny's.

The rain had stopped. Penny was watching for them and met them in the hall.

"Guess what *I've* been doing?" She grinned.

Patty was so glad to see her now, that she quite forgot she had intended to say, "I don't care!" when they next met. Together they raced to the blue room.

"*I* helped Granny tidy and dust all the things in her cabinet!" boasted Penny proudly, after Patty had made three wrong guesses.

"You mean you touched them, and *held* them, and had them all out?" gasped Patty in awe.

"Yes!" nodded Penny, "and I wore an apron and had a dear little soft brush, and a duster for the shelves. And Granny told me lovely stories about lots of the things and where they came from—and—and—and I didn't break a thing!" she finished triumphantly.

It would have been easy for Patty to feel a wave of jealousy at that moment. Such a morning seemed like a treat, not a punishment and she said so. But then, with a secret inner satisfaction, she knew that her morning had held its own private adventure, too. She told all about the visit to Miss Perdy and the tiny cluttered room, but she did not mention the portrait or the ring.

Mother was home for lunch. The twins raced to greet her and flung their arms round her neck.

"You've been good girls, I hope?" she said, kissing them. They looked at each other. For the last two hours, anyway, they thought they had.

"This afternoon I must start packing, as we go home first thing tomorrow," Mother said later. "I want you two to collect all your things and be sure that nothing is left behind."

"*Home!* Do we have to go home *already?*"

It seemed *years* since they'd left it, yet they couldn't bear to have this glorious stay come to an end. Suddenly, however, home seemed to have its attraction, too. And there would still be more than a week before school began.

"Need our dolls be packed?" they pleaded. "We *did* want to take them out this afternoon."

It was decided that Mary and Josephine might travel home in style, on their mothers' laps.

"Now I should spend a nice last afternoon in the garden, darlings," suggested Mother. "Put on your old macs. You'll find Dad and the boys out there somewhere, I think."

The girls needed no coaxing. With the dolls warmly wrapped in borrowed wool scarves they set forth full of motherly conversation and vast plans for the future. They were engrossed in their own play. Round and round about the paths they went, saving a visit to the stable as a climax to their perambulations.

"I wonder where Daddy is, and Geoff and Jim," said Penny, at last. "We haven't seen them anywhere, have we?"

As they finally neared the stable yard, they heard voices.

"Oh, I expect they are in there, cleaning that old bike," said Patty. They crossed the cobblestones to the big open door to look.

Then they stood stock-still.

A sawhorse, bits and pieces of wood, tools, a piece of rope and a paint pot were all about. Dad and Jim stood back, admiring their work, and in the middle stood Dobbin! Dobbin clean and mended! A new leg (not quite as shapely as the other one) now supported his left shoulder. A strip off someone's old fur collar was nailed on for a mane. He had had a new coat of paint and Geoff was busy unravelling a short length of rope that had been firmly glued to his behind for a tail.

"Dobbin!" cried the twins together. "You've made him all *new!*" They gazed in admiration.

"Well—not perfect," Dad was saying, "but I think it's the best we can do for now. At least he's strong enough to ride."

"Give him another twenty minutes and that paint will be dry," said Jim, testing it with his finger. "Not quite as handsomely dappled as I bet he was originally," he added, viewing his handiwork critically, with head on one side. "But not half bad, eh, Dad?"

They had obviously had a wonderful time on this project.

"This is *his* Christmas treat, isn't it?" Penny smiled, reaching up to stroke the homemade mane. "You're all clean and smart now," she whispered to the big horse.

"Oh, and you've put some new red in his nostrils, too!" admired Patty.

Before daylight faded, everyone except Dad had a turn at riding Dobbin.

"Oooh! I feel so terribly high up." Penny's voice quivered slightly, when her great moment came, for her first real ride. "Daddy, *don't* go away!"

Suddenly the floor seemed too far below, and the rafters above, dizzily near. She could even see into the hayloft, while Patty, sitting on the wheelbarrow holding the two dolls, looked like a veritable midget.

"Not *too* fast, Jim," implored Penny, clutching the horse's neck, as her brother started the rhythm of the great rockers for her.

However, when she felt accustomed to this elevated position, and found that she didn't fall off each time Dobbin plunged forward, it became more and more thrilling.

Her hair flapped in the wind, imaginary things sped by, she might have been out on the moors—riding to someone's rescue! Only reluctantly did she finally let her turn come to an end.

Inside herself, Patty had really been as scared as her sister at first, though she had been determined not to show it. It had been a magic sensation riding Dobbin.

"Well, that must be all for today," said Dad, as he finished tidying up, and Jim lifted Penny down. A dust sheet was thrown over Dobbin and they dragged him over to a corner.

"He'll be all safe and ready for you the next time you come," said Daddy, patting the hard wooden rump.

"I wonder what it must be like to ride a *real* horse?" whispered the twins.

"Joy cometh in the morning," hummed Patty happily to herself, as she lay in bed in the dark, listening to such familiar sounds as bath water running, Dad blowing his nose like a foghorn and Annie clattering around with the carpet sweeper downstairs. How hard this little bed felt. But it was "home." Yes, of course, it had been her turn for the little bed by the wall, she remembered. Every night she and Penny swapped beds because they both preferred the one by the window.

Now Patty let her mind trail back over all the delights of the Christmas holiday, reliving each special moment. Suddenly she remembered something. She slid out of bed, pulled open a drawer and reached into the back of it.

There, still intact, was that special Christmas picture she had forgotten to take. Patty lit the candle and studied it. Yes, it was pretty good, she decided, but not *nearly* so good as she had remembered it. Now she saw what more she could do to it. She would set to work today, as soon as they had written their "thank you" letters.

Patty glanced toward the other bed, where her twin was still asleep. No, she wouldn't wait, she would do it now. This could be her "thank you" letter to Granny, after all. Fastening on her dressing gown and filling the tooth glass, she got out the paints and set to work. She repainted the door-knocker on the house, making it yellow-brown. Then in two places she put a tiny blob of Chinese white. She held the picture from her, studying it intently. Yes, it *did* look more like a shiny brass knocker now. Inwardly elated, Patty began adding highlights wherever she could, even on the end of the dog's nose!

In a little while Penny woke up.

"Oh-o-o-o," she yawned. "I was just dreaming that I was having the most lovely ride on Dobbin, and I didn't want to wake up."

"*I* dreamt about the Dwarf," said Patty, a little absently, "but it was all silly and sort of mixed up."

"Shall we get the dolls up?" Penny was wide awake now. "I'm just longing to have Jennie and Dora come over to see the new members of our families, aren't you? I think the other dolls look very pleased to have such pretty new sisters. Did you notice, they'd saved some of the toffee and peppermints for them, too?"

Reluctantly Patty wrenched herself away from her painting, but not before she had accomplished several more additions and deepened the color in some places.

"That's nice," said Penny, looking over her shoulder, "but isn't that the same as one you did before?"

"Mm-m-m," grunted Patty, shaking her head. "It is, but it isn't. I've done lots more to it."

"I like that knocker. How did you make it look so real?"

"Ba-a-a-th, you kids!" Geoff pounded on their door. "Mum says it's time to dress!"

Today Patty wasn't the very last one down to breakfast. Janet was always a slow riser. But the family were all at the table, enjoying their usual banter, when the postman's knock sounded on the door, and a small cascade of letters flopped through the letter slot.

"I'll go!" Geoff bounded from his seat, to fetch the scattered envelopes from off the hall mat. "Something for everyone," he grinned, as he circled the table, sorting as he went.

"Not bills already, I hope," said Dad.

"A letter for *us*, too?" clamored the twins excitedly.

"Bags I open it!" said Patty quickly.

"Then *I* bags read it," answered Penny.

"It's from Rick!" they announced joyfully, as Penny unfolded the carefully written sheet. Then, out of the letter fell two tiny, folded paper fans. "For Mary and Josephine," the letter said.

"He's made them *himself!* And just think! He remembered their names!"

The twins beamed at these gifts, then passed the little fans round for the family to admire.

"H'm, not half bad! Jolly good!" said Jim, handing them back to the girls.

It felt as though Christmas were still going on—that wonderful Christmas at Granny's, which they hadn't wanted to end. It was still with them, even now in this familiar cosy world, where the rhythm of family life flowed safely about them, and Mum and Dad were the center of it all.